"Is there someone you would like to marry?" Tane persisted.

Euphemia wandered on a few paces and examined a charming group of miniature roses. If she said yes, he would want to know who, and if she said no, that would be a lie, and she found she couldn't tell him lies easily. "Your roses are really magnificent," she observed.

He laughed. "Put in my place, am I? Do I know him?"

She didn't quite meet his eyes. "I'm not going to answer that either."

The doctor took his hand from her arm and flung an arm around her shoulders. "I can't think why you object so strongly—after all, I have an interest in you. You're my landlady, and this man, whoever he is, might decide to buy the house, and then where should I be?"

She said earnestly, "I can promise you that won't happen," and then, forgetting everything else but his comfortable presence, she added, "He won't ever marry me. He's…he's…"

"Ah, the eternal triangle." His voice was soothing and just sufficiently impersonal, although there was a glint of laughter in his eyes. "But take heart, Phemie, there is nearly always a way out."

Romance readers around the world were sad to note the passing of **Betty Neels** in June 2001. Her career spanned thirty years, and she continued to write into her ninetieth year. To her millions of fans, Betty epitomized the romance writer, and yet she began writing almost by accident. She had retired from nursing, but her inquiring mind still sought stimulation. Her new career was born when she heard a lady in her local library bemoaning the lack of good romance novels. Betty's first book, *Sister Peters in Amsterdam*, was published in 1969, and she eventually completed 134 books. Her novels offer a reassuring warmth that was very much a part of her own personality. She was a wonderful writer, and she will be greatly missed. Her spirit and genuine talent will live on in all her stories.

THE BEST *of*
BETTY NEELS

An Apple from Eve

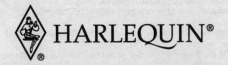

HARLEQUIN®

TORONTO • NEW YORK • LONDON
AMSTERDAM • PARIS • SYDNEY • HAMBURG
STOCKHOLM • ATHENS • TOKYO • MILAN • MADRID
PRAGUE • WARSAW • BUDAPEST • AUCKLAND

ISBN-13: 978-0-373-19927-3
ISBN-10:   0-373-19927-9

AN APPLE FROM EVE

CHAPTER ONE

IT HAD STARTED to rain fiercely and suddenly after a long dry, hot day, and the girl at the wheel of the elderly Morris 1000 halted cautiously at the traffic lights in the middle of Chiswick, listening anxiously to the puffs and wheezing of the engine—a good car on the open road, she thought loyally, but a bit of a problem in city traffic. The lights had been red for a long time; she glanced sideways at a bus drawn in close to her left and then looked to her right: a steel grey Bentley within inches of her, its driver staring ahead of him, showing her a handsome profile with an arrogant nose and a high forehead. She judged him to be a large man, although it was difficult to know that from where she was. She amused herself guessing his age; thirty-five? Forty? Younger than that perhaps, his hair was so fair that it could have been silver. He turned his head suddenly and she was disconcerted by his cold blue stare; one didn't expect complete strangers to smile at one, but neither did one expect a look of glacial dislike. She restrained herself with difficulty from the childish impulse to make a face at him, to be rendered speechless with rage as a long arm in a beautifully tailored sleeve stretched across and tapped her indicator.

'Unless you intend suicide, I suggest that you put that thing in.' His voice was as cold as his look and before she could say a word, the lights had changed and the Bentley had slipped away, out of sight in the thick traffic within seconds.

It seemed to Euphemia that she would never reach the M3, and when she did the turning to Chobham was endless miles away. She heaved a sigh of relief when she turned off at last to go through Chobham and then take the narrow road to her home, Hampton-cum-Spyway was a very small village, tucked away in a valley, with an outsize church, a cluster of picturesque cottages and a scattering of comfortably sized old houses. She went slowly down the short street, past the butchers, the baker and the post office and general stores, and drove round the village green, glimpsing old Dr Bell's car in front of her home as she turned into the gateway at the side of the house, its gate propped open for so many years now that it no longer fulfilled its function, and stopped in front of the garage.

She turned off the engine, got out and went under the rose arch in the hedge to the front garden, crossed the unkempt lawn and opened the front door. The house was charming; wisteria hung over it like a purple waterfall, almost hiding the roses sharing the walls with it, hiding too the shabby state of the paintwork. The door was solid oak studded with nails and opened into a pleasant hall. The girl went in, dropping her handbag on to a side table, stepped over a hole in the carpet with the air of one who had done it many times before, and ran upstairs two at a time.

The landing was spacious with several doors and a number of narrow passages leading in all directions. She went straight to a door at the front of the house and went in.

It was a large room, dominated by a fourposter bed and a good deal of dark oak furniture. Her father lay on the bed, his face ashen against the pillows, Dr Bell stood at the foot, Ellen, her younger sister, was standing behind him, not looking. There was a fourth person in the room bending over her father, who straightened up as she went to the bed. The driver of the Bentley.

Euphemia took her father's limp hand and smiled at him, not speaking, and it was Dr Bell who broke the silence. 'Euphemia, my dear—I'm glad you could come so quickly. A colleague of mine at St Cyprian's advised me to call in Dr van Diederijk as consultant. He's a heart specialist of international reputation.' He turned to the giant of a man standing by the bed. 'This is Euphemia Blackstock, the eldest of the Colonel's children.'

The doctor nodded and said how do you do in a politely disinterested voice. 'Can we talk somewhere?' he asked. 'The Colonel's daughters could perhaps stay with him…?'

Ellen had gone to stand by Euphemia. She was a pretty girl, fair and blue-eyed and with an air of helplessness, in direct contrast to her sister, for Euphemia was above middle height, on the plump side, with rich dark brown hair and tawny eyes and an exquisite nose above a soft too wide mouth. The mouth became surprisingly firm now. 'I should like to know what you decide,' she addressed Dr van Diederijk in a quiet voice that expected an answer.

He raised pale eyebrows. 'Of course, Miss Blackstock. You are a nurse, I believe?' Somehow he managed to convey astonishment at that fact.

'Yes.' He might be an eminent heart specialist, but she began to wonder if he had a heart himself. Reassurance and a little kindliness would have been acceptable; she had had Ellen's frightened, garbled message while she was on duty and she had driven home as fast as she could, full of forebodings. They were a close-knit family, more so since her mother had died a year previously, and they all loved their fiery-tempered, tough parent. To see him laid low on his bed had terrified Euphemia, although she hadn't allowed it to show. She wondered now if her father had been holding out on them, knowing that there was something wrong and not telling them.

She followed the two men out of the room and ignoring the consultant's cool annoyance, addressed herself to Dr Bell.

'Did Father know that he was ill? Was this unexpected? And if it wasn't why wasn't I told?'

'He expressly forbade me to mention it, Euphemia.' Dr Bell looked uncomfortable. 'A question of valves,' he went on. 'I suggested that he might put himself in the hands of a surgeon some months ago, but he wouldn't hear of it, and now it's become imperative.'

'He could recover if they operate?'

'That's for Dr van Diederijk to say.'

She turned to the silent man watching her. 'You're not a surgeon?'

'No, a physician.'

'So it's your advice which will decide whether surgery will give my father a chance.'

He nodded his splendid head. 'That is so.' He added softly: 'And now if Dr Bell and I might go somewhere undisturbed…'

She hated him; cold, arrogant, rude, self-important…

she had quite a list of adjectives by the time she was back in her father's room.

Ellen was standing forlornly looking out of the window, and Euphemia gave her a loving understanding glance as she went to the bed. Ellen had always been the baby, even though both the boys were younger than she; she hated violence and sickness, and bad temper, and Euphemia had tried to shield her from all these. It hadn't been too difficult, because Ellen had been the one to stay at home and run the house with the help of Mrs Cross who came in to oblige every day. She would have to send for the boys, thought Euphemia—just in case…

She sat down by the bed and took her father's hand again. He was too ill to talk and she made no effort to speak, sensing that peace and quiet was what he wanted. Presently she said softly to Ellen: 'Go down and make coffee, will you, darling? Those two men will want something.'

It was quite some time later when Dr Bell came back and beckoned her from the door. 'Dr van Diederijk has gone up to St Jude's—he intends to discuss your father's case with a surgeon there. He's made his decision, but he prefers to say nothing more until he's talked to Mr Crisp.'

'And you?' she asked a little sharply. 'Aren't you going to tell me anything either?'

'We must have patience, my dear,' said Dr Bell kindly, 'it's an important thing to everyone concerned.'

'When shall we know?'

Dr Bell looked awkward and she wondered why. 'At the latest tomorrow morning. Have you told the boys?'

'I'm about to telephone them.' She glanced at her watch. 'It's almost five o'clock: If I ring Stowe now they can put them on a train as soon as possible and they could be home this evening—late this evening.' She frowned a little. 'Tomorrow morning wouldn't be a better idea?' She looked past the old man. 'Father's very ill, I can see that for myself, but if they do a valve replacement...'

Dr Bell muttered something in a soothing voice. 'Travelling will be easier for them this evening—the trains are always crowded in the morning and taxis are harder to get.'

She supposed he was right, but she was too worried and unhappy to think about it. She telephoned the boys' school and was assured that they would be sent home at once. She went to find Ellen, sent her to the kitchen to coax Mrs Cross to stay a bit later and get a meal ready, then went herself to her father's room where Dr Bell was standing by his patient's bed. 'I have evening surgery,' he told her, 'but I'll come the moment you want me. I'm afraid there's nothing much we can do until we have the consultants' opinions.'

Euphemia drew up a chair and sat down beside her father, sleeping peacefully, a drugged sleep, but she was thankful for it; he wasn't a man to bear with illness and she couldn't have borne to have seen him lying there worrying about himself. Presently Ellen came in with a supper tray.

'I'll take over when you say so,' she whispered, but, Euphemia shook her head.

'I'm not tired, you stay downstairs and make sure everything is ready for the boys. Oh, and be a dear and ring St Cyprian's and tell them that I can't come back tonight—explain, will you? I'll telephone them in the morning.'

Dr Bell came again much later. The Colonel was still unconscious and beyond taking his pulse he did nothing.

'Shouldn't he go to hospital?' asked Euphemia urgently.

'Dr van Deiderijk thinks it unwise to move him for the moment.'

She looked at the kind elderly face she had known for all of twenty years. 'If you say so…' She sighed. 'If you hear anything from that man you'll let me know at once— won't you?'

'Of course. You don't like him, my dear?'

'No,' said Euphemia flatly.

The boys got home late that night and in the early hours of the morning her father died. Euphemia, sitting with him, didn't call them from their beds; there was no point in doing so. Dr Bell came in answer to her telephone call, and surprisingly, Dr van Diederijk came with him. It was almost five o'clock now and a pearly morning that promised to be a warm day, and beside Dr Bell's hastily dragged on clothes, the Dutchman's appearance suggested that he had been up, freshly shaved, and immaculately dressed after a long restful night.

Euphemia greeted them with a face stony with fiercely held back grief. It was later, downstairs in the shabby sitting-room, that she asked:

'Was it your decision not to admit my father to hospital, Dr van Diederijk?'

He was standing before the fireplace, his hands in his pockets.

'Yes.'

'Why?' She took a breath and went on in a rush: 'You took away his only chance! What right had you to do that—he might be alive now if you'd advised operation…'

'Alive, yes, if you can call it living to be attached to

monitoring machines and drips and ECGs. Your father was an intelligent man, he would have been only too aware that he was being kept alive but with no hope of leading a normal life again. It would have been a matter of days only—can you imagine what that would have meant to him? You must know in your heart that I made the right decision—he had been ill for a long time, I understand— far too long for a replacement to be satisfactory. Besides, he wasn't a young man any more…'

'Then why wasn't I told?' Her voice shook with rage and grief.

'I have it from Dr Bell that he didn't wish you to be told.' He looked at the other man, who nodded.

Euphemia turned her back on them both so that they shouldn't see the tears. In a moment when she had control of her voice she said: 'If I'd known, I could have stayed at home and nursed him.'

'For that very reason he wished nothing to be said. I must say that I can understand his wishes; you must try and understand too.'

She spun round to face him. 'Well, I don't, but then I'm not made of ice…he was my father, you know—and even if he weren't I wouldn't be so cold-blooded about it as you are!'

She rushed out of the room, brushing past him, one small corner of her numbed brain aware of the faint whiff of expensive aftershave as she did so. She went to the kitchen, made herself a pot of tea, had a hearty cry and pulled herself together. It was all of twenty minutes by the time she had made her way back to the shabby, comfort-able sitting-room. The two men were there, waiting patiently, and she asked them in a wooden voice if they would like coffee. She looked a fright by now, her beautiful nose red with weeping, her eyelids swollen, but she really didn't care. When they refused, she enquired politely if there was anything else to be done, and when Dr Bell told her that he would make all the necessary arrangements, accompanied them to the door and bade them good morning, remarking on the beauty of the day as she did so. Dr Bell patted her shoulder, said he'd be back later and made for his car, while Dr van Diederijk paused on the doorstep. 'Give yourself a double whisky and go and lie down for a couple of hours,' he advised her. 'It will help you to get through the day.'

She didn't answer him, only gave him a cold glance and went indoors. All the same, she did as he had said. The whisky went straight to her head; she prudently set the alarm for eight o'clock and got on to her bed and fell instantly asleep.

The man was right, she had to admit later. She awoke refreshed and clear-headed, able to tackle the day ahead of her, full of so many problems. It was at the end of it that she began to think about the future. The boys would be all right; their school fees would be covered by a fund their father had set up for them years ago. She herself would be able to keep herself easily enough, but Ellen was a different matter. She couldn't remain at home by herself, but on the other hand she had had no particular training. Euphemia frowned over the problem and then decided to ask Mr Fish their solicitor's advice.

She had only the vaguest notion of her father's income; there had never been much money and the house had grown shabby with the years, but he had lived comfortably and money had been something he had never discussed with her. She dismissed the matter and set herself to writing to various relations and friends. The boys she had sent to stay with friends close by for a couple of days and Ellen was of no use at all, declaring that she couldn't possibly think of anything except her father's death. Euphemia had comforted her gently and sent her to bed early, staying up late herself, writing her letters until, quite worn out, she went to bed herself.

She got through the following days with outward calm. She was a girl with plenty of common sense, and it stood her in good stead now. She loved her father and she grieved for him, but life had to go on. He would have been the first to remind her of that.

Aunts, uncles and cousins she barely knew came to the funeral, and when Aunt Thea, a mild-looking middle-aged lady with a deplorable taste in hats, suggested with genuine eagerness that Ellen should go back to Middle Wallop with her for a long visit, Euphemia thanked heaven silently for settling one of her most pressing problems. The boys were going back to school on the following day and she would return to the Men's Medical ward at St Cyprian's on the day after that. There only remained the reading of her father's will, and that would hold no surprises.

She couldn't have been more mistaken. Sitting in the small room the Colonel had used as his study, watching Mr Fish gather together his papers after the will had been read, Euphemia tried to take it all in and failed. She hadn't expected there would be much money, but she had never guessed at debts, still less that the house—their loved home—was mortgaged and would have to be sold. Mr Fish had been adamant about that; either she must lay her hands on the very considerable sum the house was worth, or sell it and pay off the mortgage. People, said Mr Fish in his dry, elderly voice, tended to be businesslike about such things. The fact that they were rendering someone homeless was secondary to their instinct for good business.

'Don't worry, I'll think of something,' Euphemia promised her brothers and sister. 'No one's going to do anything for a month at least, there's plenty of time to fix something up.' She spoke so cheerfully that they actually believed her.

'Uncle Tom—would he lend us the money?' asked Ellen hopefully, and, 'Cousin Fred drove here in a socking great Jag,' observed Nicky, the elder of her brothers.

'But he's getting married,' Billy, the youngest, chimed in, and added with all the wisdom of twelve years, 'He'll need all his money.'

Euphemia swept them all to their feet. 'Well, we're not going to worry about it now, Father wouldn't have liked it. Ellen, shouldn't you go and pack, and you two, put out what you need and I'll pop up presently.'

She went back to the drawing-room where the last of the family were bidding each other goodbye. They met seldom, only at christenings or weddings or funerals, when they enjoyed a good gossip. Dr Bell was still there too. Euphemia whispered: 'I want to speak to you,' as she went past him, and when the last of her relatives, barring Aunt Thea who had gone to help Ellen pack, had disappeared through the open gate, she turned to him.

'Dr Bell, I want your advice. Father has left some

debts—not many, but they must be paid, and the house is mortgaged. Mr Fish says we must sell it, but…well, it's our home. There must be another way of getting the money, only I can't think of it at the moment.'

He beamed at her, pleased that he could help. 'There is another way—at least, you can postpone selling the house for a time. Find a tenant, and let it furnished. I believe that might bring in enough to pay the instalments on the mortgage. I'm not going to say it's the right answer, but it would give you a breathing space, and who knows, something may happen…'

'You mean win a prize from Ernie or marry a millionaire?' She beamed at him. 'Dr Bell, you're an angel! That's what I'll do. How do I start? Advertise? And how much rent should I ask?' She faltered for a moment. 'If only Father…' She blinked back tears and smiled again, a shaky, lopsided smile this time. 'Bless you for thinking of it, Dr Bell.'

He patted her arm. 'As I said, it may serve its purpose for a breathing space while you all get adjusted. I'll ask around—I meet a good many people, someone somewhere will be looking for just such a place as this.'

Ellen and Aunt Thea joined them then and when they had driven off, Ellen tearful but happy to have her immediate future settled for her, Euphemia bade the doctor goodbye and went up to the boys' room to help them pack. The house seemed very quiet and empty, and would be even more so presently when they had gone. She got out the car and drove them to the station and stood waving until the train was out of sight.

It was getting dark when she got back to the house, with

an overcast sky and the threat of thunder. She made herself
a pot of tea and ate some of the leftover sandwiches, then
went along to her father's study to start sorting out the
papers in his desk. Her sadness had gone beyond tears; she
felt numb, anxious to get as much done as possible before
she went back to the hospital in the morning. She worked
until late into the night and then wandered through the nice
old house, wondering if she would be able to let it at a good
rent, whether she would ever have the chance to pay off
the mortgage; it was for a frighteningly large amount. She
was still doing sums in her head when she fell asleep in
the pretty bedroom she had had since she was a small girl.

She had been dreading returning to the hospital. She had
a great many friends there; she had done her training with
most of them, worked her way up the ladder of promotion
until she had been offered Men's Medical two years previously, and now at the age of twenty-seven, she had a safe
future before her. Not that she wished to remain a nurse
for ever; she wanted to marry, preferably a man with
enough money to support her in comfort somewhere in the
country—a garden, she had daydreamed idly from time to
time, with a donkey and dogs and children to play in it. But
none of these things would be of any use unless she loved
him and he loved her.

Driving to work through the early morning she realised
that her vague dreams would have to go by the board for
the present. Ellen had to be thought of, and the boys. No
man in his right mind would be prepared to take on a
whole family, and even if she succeeded in finding
someone to rent their home she would have to go on
working. She could see no chance of ever paying the

mortgage off, but with each year of instalments paid, there was the chance that something might happen. She turned the car into the hospital forecourt and parked neatly. As she crossed to the swing doors she decided that Ellen would probably marry someone rich who would want to live in the house and thus keep it in the family—a childish notion but comforting none the less.

Everyone was very kind to her. The Senior Nursing Officer, a tart middle-aged lady who seldom had a kind word for anyone, was surprisingly sympathetic, and Euphemia's own friends lingered on their way to their wards to offer their sympathy. And once on her own ward, her nurses, who liked her because she was sensible and fair and kind as well as very pretty, made it their business to murmur conventional stilted phrases. It was the tray of tea on her desk and the vase of flowers beside it that touched her; they might not have known quite what to say to her, but the tea spoke volumes.

And the patients knew all about it too, all of them, from crabby old Mr Crouch, who disliked everyone on principle, to Dicky, the boy with a heart condition, six feet tall but with the mind of a four-year-old. As she did her morning round, Euphemia received sympathy from each one of the twenty-four beds' occupants.

She had been prepared for it, but she found that by the end of the day she was worn out. She went off duty finally, made tea; had a long hot bath and went along to telephone Ellen, who it seemed had settled in nicely, although grieving in her gentle way and anxious to know what was to be done about their home. Euphemia reassured her firmly and went back to her room to write to the boys. By the time she had done that she was tired; another pot of tea with her friends coming off their evening duty, and she was ready for bed. She hadn't expected to sleep, but she did.

Sir Richard Blake, doing his weekly round the next morning, had something to say too. He considered her a sensible girl, with no nonsense about her, and he had been acquainted with the Colonel. He swept round the ward barking questions at the students trailing behind him, leaving them limp at the ward doors when he had finished, although his patients, to whom he showed nothing but benevolence, regretted to see him go. But he didn't leave immediately. Euphemia, bidding him good morning and speeding him on his way with a polite 'Thank you, sir,' was surprised when he marched into her office with a brusque: 'A minute of your time, Sister.'

She followed him in and closed the door, trying hard to remember if she had done anything awful since his last round.

'Sorry to hear about your father.' The brusqueness hid sympathy. 'He was a splendid man.' Sir Richard went over to the window and stood with his back to her, looking out at the dreary side street it over-looked. 'Dr Bell mentioned that you were thinking of letting the house for a while— seems a good idea—very nice place you've got there, ideal for someone who wants peace and quiet. As a mater of fact I've mentioned it to someone, he'll probably get in touch…'

Euphemia addressed the elderly back, aware that Sir Richard was feeling uncomfortable and probably afraid that she might burst into tears.

'That's very kind of you, sir, and I'm very grateful. It seems the best thing to do until we've had time to discuss things…' She wasn't going to tell him that it was in fact the only thing to do. 'I think Father would have approved—there's no one to run the house at present and it would be a shame for it to stay empty.'

Her companion went to the door. 'You're probably right. You're a sensible young woman.' He coughed. 'No use being sentimental, glad to see you taking it so well.' He opened the door. 'I'll be half an hour later for next week's round, by the way.'

Euphemia went and sat at her desk, for the moment oblivious of the ward just outside the door.

He had believed her, she thought; no one need know that there wasn't a penny piece in the family kitty and that the house was mortgaged up to the chimeypots. For the first time since her father's death she felt cheerful. They would all miss their home abominably, but they were all young; Ellen was barely twenty and would certainly marry and the boys—well, their education at least was safe, and Nicky would go into the Army, probably Billy would too. As for herself... A knock on the door and her staff nurse's head poked round it stopped her brooding: old Mr Steele was a very nasty colour and would Sister take a look at him?

The days dragged, although they were busy too. She had deliberately changed her days off so that she could work, but now she was free for two days, and just as deliberately she had arranged to go and see Ellen on the first of them and then spend the night at home before embarking on the task of packing up their personal possessions. She had heard no more about a possible tenant; she would have to go to a house agent and put it in their hands.

She was sitting in her office making out the Kardex before she went off duty when one of the student nurses knocked on the door, said: 'There's someone to see you, Sister,' and went away again. Euphemia, head bowed over her report, muttered: 'OK—who is it?' and then looked up blankly at Dr van Diederijk's suave voice: 'You will forgive me, Sister, but we have an urgent matter to discuss and I am a busy man.'

'I'm quite busy too,' observed Euphemia promptly, 'and I'm going off duty at any minute now.'

This contradictory remark caused him to smile thinly, but he didn't waste words on it. 'I should like to rent your house; I hear from Sir Richard Blake that you propose to let it for a period. If you will let me have the name of your solicitor and the rent you are asking the matter should be settled without delay.'

She reviewed mixed feelings. Relief that here was a chance to rent the house quickly and offer respite from the foreclosure of the mortgage, surprise at seeing the man again, and a deep annoyance that it should be he who wanted to live in her home. 'Why the hurry?' she asked matter-of-factly.

He gave her an impatient look. 'It is hardly your business, is it? But since you are curious enough to ask...I come very frequently to London; I am a consultant in several hospitals here and I need somewhere quiet to live. Does that satisfy you?'

Euphemia said sweetly: 'If it satisfies my solicitor, it will satisfy me.'

'What rent had you in mind?'

She stared at him silently; she had no idea. After a few moments she said so, and seethed at the thin smile he gave her. 'Perhaps that should be left for your solicitor to decide?' he suggested. 'I had thought…' He named a sum which made her catch her breath—more than enough to cover the mortgage repayments; almost twice as much as she had hoped to get.

She said sharply: 'Isn't that a great deal too much?' and got another mocking smile.

'You may be an excellent nurse, Miss Blackstock, but I fear you are no business woman. Your house is worth that amount to me and I think that your solicitor will not dispute that.'

'But you said you weren't going to live there all the time?'

'My home is in Holland, nevertheless I prefer to have a second home here, at least for the foreseeable future. I intend to marry shortly and it will be convenient—I can hardly expect my wife to live in hotels.'

She was diverted by the idea of him marrying; he wasn't all that young—late thirties, she judged, perhaps younger, it was difficult to tell. She had thought of him as married and had felt vaguely sorry for his wife. She wondered what his fiancée was like, tall and slim and ethereal and as cool as he was, probably… She was recalled to her surroundings by his voice, impatient again. 'I take it that you have no objection if I view the house.'

'None at all.'

'Then may I come tomorrow? In the afternoon, if possible, and it would be convenient if you were there, so that any small problems could be dealt with at once.'

'It's my day off…'

'I know.' His tone implied that she had made a silly remark.

It would be lovely, she thought, to tell him that she had

changed her mind and wasn't going to rent her home after all. She dismissed the idea immediately; it didn't really matter who lived there, just as long as her home remained in the family. She said quietly: 'Very well, Doctor, would three o'clock suit you?'

He went then, after a brief goodbye. The little room seemed very empty, but then he was such a very large man.

CHAPTER TWO

Euphemia made short work of the Kardex, handed over to Sue Baker, her staff nurse, and hurried off duty. She would have to change her plans; she would go home straight away, polish, dust and Hoover and arrange a vase or two of flowers. She supposed she would have to give Dr van Diederijk tea; that would mean cleaning the silver tea service and getting out the china tea things they only used on great occasions. Well, it was hardly a great occasion, she argued to herself as she flung off her uniform, but she had no intention of allowing even the faintest whiff of poverty to reach the doctor's splendid nose.

She got into a cotton dress and packed the expensive cotton jersey she had bought only last month and then rummaged in her cupboard to find the sandals that went with it, her mind busy with the chores which lay ahead of her. She must ring Ellen before she left the hospital and put off seeing her until the following day, and if there was enough of everything in the larder, she might make some little cakes for tea.

She toyed with the idea of bribing Mrs Cross to come

over and serve it, but perhaps that would be a bit obvious—one could try too hard.

Polishing the hall table a couple of hours later, she found herself glad to have so much to do. She had been dreading coming home to a house without her father, but she had had no time to sit and broad. The nice old place had a neglected air with no one living in it, already it was beginning to come alive again, although there was still a good deal to be done. Euphemia had opened all the windows the moment she got in and Hoovered like mad because she had the feeling that he was the kind of man to ask her, ever so politely, to open this or that door so that he might see what was behind it. There were several bedrooms which hadn't been used for months, so she raced around making them presentable with counterpanes and a brisk dusting. Several of the cupboards were stuffed with the boys' things, too, as well as Ellen's and her last year's clothes, but these she decided, he would have to accept; they could be cleared out later.

She went to bed late after a sketchy supper and was up betimes, arranging flowers, polishing once more, turning the shabby rugs to hide the threadbare patches. Breakfast was as sketchy as her supper had been because she still had the cakes to make. She finished her housework, spent half an hour searching for the back door key, which no one had ever bothered about, and went to the kitchen to do her baking. There was time to make a fruit cake too and everything she needed to make it with. With everything safely in the oven she went upstairs, changed into the pale green jersey and the sandals, did her hair in a rather careless knot at the back of her head, made up her pretty face and went downstairs once more. The little cakes were done, and very nice they looked too. Euphemia made herself some coffee while she waited for the fruit cake to bake to perfection, arranged it on the Spode china plate, and walked across the green to the pub, where she ate fish and chips in the basket with a splendid appetite before going back to put the final touches to the tea tray.

She had planned to be in the garden, sitting at her ease with a book, when the doctor arrived, but she was doing her face once again when he thumped the knocker. He was early—wanting to catch her out, she thought crossly as she raced downstairs to open the door, so that her 'Good afternoon, Dr van Diederijk' was coldly said.

'I'm early,' his eyes searched her face, 'and you're annoyed about it. Would you like me to go away for half an hour?'

She pinkened with embarrassment. 'No, of course not—it doesn't matter in the least. Please come in,' and because she felt guilty of bad manners she pointed out the torn carpet in a kindly way.

He stepped over the hole neatly. 'I had noticed it,' he told her. 'A good carpet too—a Moorfields, isn't it? You could have it repaired.'

She didn't choose to answer this; anything could be repaired provided there was the money to pay for it. She asked haughtily: 'Where would you like to start?'

He didn't answer her at once but crossed the hall to take a leisurely look at the portrait hanging on the father wall. It had been done years previously as a surprise Christmas present for her father—her mother, Ellen, the boys and herself, painted in a charming group against the background of the oak-panelled wall in the sitting room.

The doctor said, to surprise her: 'I hope you will leave that—it belongs to the house, doesn't it?'

'Well, if you don't mind, I will—I haven't anywhere to hang it…'

He turned to look at her. 'I understand from Sir Richard that your sister will be living with an aunt—do you intend to do the same?'

It really wasn't any business of his, but if she annoyed him he might not rent the house from her. 'No, I shall stay at the hospital,' and to forestall the next question: 'The boys will go to my aunt for their holidays.' She opened the drawing-room door, because that was the grandest room in the house even if shabby. She had polished and dusted and put flowers in the vases and it looked charming and welcoming too. The doctor wandered in and strolled around, asking none of the questions she had expected. 'It's an open fire,' she pointed out unnecessarily, 'and there's a radiator under the end window—the central heating isn't very modern, but it works.'

He nodded, went past her and opened the door on to the garden. He stood on the patio outside, still not speaking, and her heart sank. The garden was large, hedged with beech, its flower beds a riot of colour; it was also unkempt, its grass too long, weeds everywhere. Euphemia said quickly: 'The garden will be tidied up before you—that is—if you take the house.'

'Did I not make it plain that I would rent it from you?' He gave her a cool enquiring look. 'I will arrange for a gardener. Is there anyone who will housekeep? Perhaps you know of a good woman?'

'There's Mrs Cross, she came in each day while

my…she's a widow and lives just across the green, she's got a sister who lives close by—she came in to help with spring-cleaning. I daresay she might work for you as well—it's a large house for one, although I don't suppose you'll be using all the rooms.'

He wasn't going to answer that either, but turned from the door. 'Perhaps we might look at them?'

She showed him the sitting-room, shabbier than any other room in the house because they had all used it whenever they were at home, and then her father's study and lastly the morning-room which was in fact a repository for fishing rods, tennis racquets, an elderly sewing machine and a catholic selection of books on the shelves which ran along one wall.

'I shall clear all this away,' said Euphemia, and he nodded.

The kitchen with the pantry beyond, a stillroom and what had once been the game larder was inspected quickly; he merely stood in the middle of the floor and observed: 'If Mrs Cross is satisfied with this, I need not bother too much. Upstairs?'

She led him up the staircase and in and out of the bedrooms, most of them agreeably roomy, the smaller ones at the back of the house making up for their lack of size by their plain washed walls and plaster cornices. They were sparsely furnished, but what there was was old and graceful and, thanks to Euphemia's hard work, beautifully polished.

Back on the main landing again, the doctor spoke. 'Two bathrooms, you said?'

It sounded quite inadequate in a house of that size. 'There's a shower in the bathroom at the front of the house,' offered Euphemia, unaware how anxious her voice sounded.

He agreed smoothly. 'You have no objection to me having another shower put in—there's a small dressing room adjoining this room...' He strode across and opened a door and when she followed meekly: 'At my expense, of course.'

'If you want one,' she conceded. Why a man living alone should need two bathrooms and two showers was beyond her, even if this fiancée of his came visiting, unless she was the kind of girl who brought Mum with her...she very nearly giggled and he threw her an enquiring glance. 'You are amused?' he wanted to know.

'No, no, of course not. Is there anywhere else you would like to go? Then perhaps you would like a cup of tea?'

'Thank you, that would be welcome. I'll get in touch with my solicitor tomorrow and you will be hearing from yours shortly. I should like to move in within the next ten days.'

Euphemia's mind boggled at the amount of packing up to be done in that time. She would have to get Ellen to help her and perhaps Mrs Cross, and as though he had read her thoughts: 'May I suggest that your—er—personal possessions should be stored in one of the bedrooms—it will give you a great deal less work. I should be obliged if the morning room could be cleared so that my secretary will have a room in which to work.'

'Yes, of course. Will she live here too?'

His tone withered her. 'What a singularly stupid question, Miss Blackstock!'

She pinkened. 'Yes, it was,' she agreed cheerfully. 'So sorry, I forgot that you're engaged.'

'And that is equally stupid.'

'Ah, now there you're wrong,' she told him cheerfully. 'If I were going to marry you I'd take grave exception to a secretary living in the house with you.'

'God forbid!' He gave her a nasty mocking smile. 'That you were going to marry me.'

Euphemia's tawny eyes shone with rage. 'And I'll say amen to that,' she told him sweetly. 'Shall we go downstairs? If you will go into the drawing-room I'll bring in the tea.'

She sailed into the kitchen, put the kettle on and warmed the teapot. The tea tray looked very nice—paper-thin china, the silver spoons, silver hot water jug and sugar bowl, the little cakes piled appetisingly on to Sèvres china. Euphemia bounced to the table and took one and bit into it. 'And I hope they choke him!' she declared in a loud cross voice.

'In which case he won't be able to rent the house, will he?' enquired the doctor's gentle voice. He was standing just inside the door, not smiling, although she had the impression that he was deeply amused about something. 'I came to see if I could carry the tray…'

'How kind—it's this one.' She ladled the tea into he pot without looking at him, and made the tea. When she looked round he had gone again with the tray.

She would have to apologise, she supposed, but in this she was frustrated, for each time she opened her mouth to do so, her companion made some remark which required a proper answer. It wasn't long before she realised that he was doing it deliberately, keeping the conversation strictly businesslike, asking her about local tradespeople and then getting up to leave once he'd got all the answers. She accompanied him to the door and wished him a polite goodbye.

'The little cakes were delicious,' he told her. 'Far too light to choke upon. Good day to you, Miss Blackstock.'

Euphemia stood in the open doorway, staring after him as he climbed into his Bentley and drove away. Part of her mind registered the fact that he did this with a calm skill and careless ease, just as though he were mounting a bicycle. 'Oh, blow the man!' she said under her breath, and went in to clear the tea things.

Later that evening she telephoned Aunt Thea and told her the news, and that lady, a woman of good sense, agreed that it was a splendid solution to rent the house and did Euphemia want Ellen there to help pack up?

'That's the doctor who came to see Father,' said Ellen unnecessarily into the phone presently. 'Then he must be a nice man.'

'Why?' asked Euphemia baldly.

'Well, to like our house enough to want to live in it.'

A viewpoint Euphemia hadn't considered. 'He's taking it for a year.' She told her sister, 'He wants to come in ten days' time. Aunt Thea suggested that you might come up and help pack up our things, but there's no need. I'll get Mrs Cross and we can put everything in one of the bedrooms and lock the door.'

'Oh, you mustn't do that!' Ellen sounded quite horri-fied. 'It looks as if you don't trust him.'

'Rubbish,' declared Euphemia, rather struck with the idea all the same. 'I'm sure it's the usual thing to do.'

'Oh, well—' Ellen sounded uncertain. 'We wouldn't want to upset him.'

'Nothing would upset him,' said Euphemia snappily, so that Ellen said instantly:

'Are you sure you don't want me to help pack up?'

'No, love—I'll start tomorrow and finish on my days off next week. Are you happy, Ellen?'

'Aunt Thea is a dear, it's funny being here after—after home and Father, but I'm happy, Phemie, really I am. Are you all right?'

'Yes, love. I'll telephone in a day or two.'

Euphemia spent the whole of the next day collecting up the small personal possessions of them all and it was only half done by the time she left that evening, even so the house didn't look the same without the clutter of tennis racquets and cricket bats and Ellen's collection of paperweights, and the pot plants she had tended so carefully. Euphemia moved them all into the greenhouse because she didn't think that the doctor would care to have the task of watering them regularly—she must remember to ask Mrs Cross to do something about that.

The ward was busy when she got back to the hospital, too busy for her to indulge in her own private thoughts, and her free time was almost entirely taken up with visits to Mr Fish and the house agents. They were all entirely satisfactory, and she felt almost lighthearted as she drove down to Hampton-cum-Spyway for her days off.

Mrs Cross had been in her absence; the hall was freshly polished and the windows and paintwork gleamed. It was the same in the sitting-room and the drawing-room, and in the kitchen she found a note written in Mrs Cross's spidery writing to the effect that she had done downstairs and would be back again to give upstairs the same treatment after Miss Phemie had finished packing up, and there was milk in the fridge.

Euphemia made tea, ate the doughnuts she had bought on her way home, and rolled up her sleeves. In five days the doctor would be taking up residence and there must be no trace of the family Blackstock left in the house. She worked until late, got up early in the morning and went on packing, pausing only for a quick meal at the pub and a brief visit to Mrs Cross who on the strength of her new job and, Euphemia suspected, more money, had brought a bright blue nylon overall and had her hair permed.

'Every day 'e wants me,' she explained. 'Got to get 'is breakfast most mornings and cook 'im a meal at night, but 'e's almost never 'ome for 'is lunch and I'm ter suit meself 'ow I'm ter work. Me sister Eth, she'll come in mornings and give an 'and. Paying us 'andsome, 'e is, too.'

'That's very nice for you, Mrs Cross,' said Euphemia cheerfully, and her companion made hasty to add: 'Not but I wasn't 'appy with you an' yer father. I'll miss yer…'

'Well, yes, we've all had to make changes, haven't we?' She kept her voice steady. 'But it's nice that we can keep the house this way, and Dr van Diederijk seems to like it.'

'But 'e won't be 'ere all the time, 'e goes 'ome ter'. Holland quite a bit. I gets me pay whether 'e's here or not.'

'That's splendid, Mrs Cross. Now, I must go—I've still an awful lot to do. You've got the back door key, haven't you? I'll keep mine until the doctor actually gets here just in case there's something I've forgotten.'

Euphemia went back to the house and began on the boys' rooms—the worst of the lot, what with model trains and boats and footballs all over the place. By the end of the second day she was tired out but satisfied. The house looked delightful—shabby, certainly, but the furniture was good and well polished and she had decided that somehow or other she would come down and arrange fresh flowers. Mrs Cross had offered to do it, but she tended to fling a dozen blooms into a vase and leave it at that. The roses in the garden were flowering well; she would pick the choicest. On the thought she went and gathered a bunch for herself to take back to her room; after all, the house wasn't the doctor's for another five days.

She managed to give herself a free evening on the day before he was due to move in, and drove herself down through a heavy summer shower to spend an hour or more gathering roses and arranging them around the house. As she made a last tour of inspection the thought struck her forcibly that now the house was no longer home. Until then, polishing and cleaning and turning out cupboards, she hadn't allowed herself to think of that, but now she would have no right to come any more; she would have to travel down to Middle Wallop or spend her free days window shopping and going to cinemas. She came slowly out of the drawing-room, her eyes full of tears, but not bothering with them, since there was no one to see her crying, and lifted the latch of the front door. It was opened at the same time from outside and she found herself staring up into the doctor's face.

Without giving any reason as to why he was there, he pushed her gently back into the hall and came in and shut the door. 'This is still your home. I've only borrowed it for a time.' He smiled so kindly at her that she could only gape at him, astonished that he had hit the nail on the head so unerringly. He went on matter-of-factly: 'Is everything locked up and put away, or can we have a cup of coffee? I was on my way back from a patient of mine in Guildford and it seemed an idea to come this way. I didn't expect to find anyone here.' His eyes had taken in the bowl of roses on the side table. 'Flowers,' he observed, 'and a wonderful smell of polish and lavender bags. Thank you, specially as you had no need to do it.'

Euphemia sniffed. 'I wasn't going to hand it over all dusty and—and lonely.' She got out a hanky and blew her nose vigorously and wiped her eyes. 'I'll get some coffee.'

They went into the kitchen together and she made coffee for them both while he carried on a rather one-sided conversation about nothing in particular. They left the house together presently, and he gave her no chance to linger but ushered her through the door with a brisk: 'Of course, you will be coming back, probably sooner than you think.'

Euphemia had murmured something, intent on being sensible and unsentimental about it all, then got into the Morris and driven away after bidding him goodbye in answer to his own still brisk farewell. He had been kind, she acknowledged, as she started on the drive back to the hospital, but she still didn't like him. And why had he been there, anyway? He hadn't told her that. She shrugged the thought aside; it didn't matter now, in a few hours he would be living there. She wanted to cry again because she was lonely and missed her father, and picking up the threads of life and changing its pattern wouldn't be easy.

She flung herself into her work with an energy which left her nurses breathless, and even Sir Richard, pausing at the end of his round to bid her a courteous farewell, remarked that her devotion to duty exceeded even his high standards. 'But I daresay you are glad to be occupied,' he observed, 'although it must be a great relief to you to know that Dr van Diederijk is your tenant at Hampton-cum-Spyway and not some stranger.'

Euphemia clenched her teeth on the observation that he was, at any rate to her, a complete stranger. She agreed politely and sped the great man on his way to the Women's Medical. But it was a relief all the same when the cheque for the handsome sum Dr van Diederijk was paying every month arrived by the next day's post. She paid it into the bank with instructions that the mortgage was to be paid each month. There was still a little money over: holidays, she decided, clothes for the boys, and perhaps it would pay for some sort of training for Ellen, only she wasn't sure what. Of course, Ellen might marry. She had had a number of boy-friends, although Euphemia didn't think that she was serious about any of them; all the same it was a very likely possibility.

Euphemia stopped thinking about Ellen for a moment and thought about herself. Matthew Patterson, whose parents lived on the other side of the green, had asked her to marry him several times, but she had refused him on each occasion; his eyes were too close together, she considered, and he had a nasty temper. And there was Terry Walker too, Senior Medical Registrar, who had proposed, rather lightheartedly, she had to admit—besides, she had the lowering feeling that when he discovered her father had left them all without a penny, he wouldn't be as keen as he made out. Miss Blackstock, with a highly respected colonel for a father and a supposedly comfortable portion of his worldly goods to come her way sooner or later, was a rather different kettle of fish from Miss Blackstock with nothing at all. But it was hardly fair to think about herself; it was the boys who mattered. The house would have gone to Nicky and she must at all costs try and save it for him. The sums she had scribbled on the backs of envelopes and scraps of paper weren't encouraging; the mortgage would take fifteen years to pay off, which would be about right for Nicky but would leave her, at the ripe age of forty-two, exactly where she was now...

It was almost a week later when she received a brief note from Dr van Diederijk inviting her to join himself and a few friends for drinks at her old home. In four days' time, he had written in a rather sprawling hand, and underlined the date and the time. She read it several times and then put it down on her desk as Terry Walker walked in.

He was a good-looking youngish man, ambitious and good at his work but not over-liked by his colleagues. He smiled at her now in a rather guarded manner and asked: 'What's this I hear about you renting your house? Surely you'll need to keep it open for the boys and your sister?' And when she didn't answer at once: 'You didn't have to rent it, did you?' He gave her a sharp look and although she hadn't meant to tell him anything she changed her mind now.

'Yes, we did. The house is mortgaged.'

He looked so surprised that she felt quite sorry for him. 'You mean you've no money?' At her cold stare he added hastily: 'What I mean is, how about the boys—their education?'

'That's safe enough.' She saw the embarrassment on his face and felt sorry for him—after all, he had been home with her once or twice and he must have got the impression that her background was comfortable and solid. To lighten the atmosphere she picked up the letter. 'I've had an invitation to have drinks in my own home, don't you think that was nice of Dr van Diederijk?'

Terry read it quickly. 'Good lord, you're not going? Can't you see he's only being polite? I don't imagine for one moment he expects you to go. He couldn't do less than ask you, of course, knowing that you won't accept.'

Euphemia kept her eyes on the desk, which was a good thing, because they glittered like topazes. She said softly: 'No, of course not,' a remark which could have meant a lot or nothing at all. As she got up to accompany Terry on his round, she was already planning what she should wear.

She took care to get to Hampton-cum-Spyway a little late. The last thing she wanted was a *tête-à-tête* with her host, and she had timed it well. There were a number of cars strung out around the green and lights in all the downstairs windows. As she rang the bell she could hear the discreet hum of conversation coming from the drawing-room.

Mrs Cross opened the door, wearing the blue overall and looking important. 'Oh, it's you, Miss Euphemia—you could have walked in—it's your 'ouse.' She smiled briefly. 'I'm ever so busy.'

'I'm sure you are,' agreed Euphemia, 'but I couldn't really walk in, now could I?' She went to the mirror above the wall table and tucked away a strand of hair. She had taken pains to make the most of herself and the dress she was wearing, while not new, was an expensive one her father had given her on her last birthday; finely pleated chiffon over a silk slip, very simply cut, its blues and greens and tawny shades making the most of her eyes.

'And very nice, too,' commented Dr van Diederijk from the drawing-room door. 'I was beginning to think that you weren't coming.'

She held out her hand. 'There was a good deal of traffic…' She gave him a social smile and was annoyed to see that he was looking amused, but he replied gravely enough: 'It was good of you to come.'

They crossed the hall together. 'Well, I was curious,' she told him frankly, and was put out at his bland: 'Yes, I thought you might be.'

The drawing-room was full. At first glance Euphemia was reassured to see a number of faces she already knew, but there were an equal number of people she had never seen before. Dr van Diederijk touched her arm lightly and introduced her to a small group of people, several of whom she knew slightly, waited long enough to see that she had a glass of sherry and then moved away. She exchanged small talk for ten minutes or so and then, catching sight of Dr Bell, excused herself and made her way over to him.

'I'm so glad you're here,' she told him. 'I don't know half these people.' She took another sherry from a passing waiter and took an appreciative sip, quite forgetting that she'd missed her tea and supper was unlikely.

'You're all right, my dear?' asked Dr Bell kindly.

Euphemia smiled a little tremulously because his sympathy was real and she had grown tired of presenting a calm face to so many people who had asked the same question without really wanting to know. 'Yes, we're managing. It'll get better, won't it? Just at first… Ellen's settled down very well, I'm going down my next days off to see her. The boys are fine too. It's such a relief that the house is let.' She drank the rest of her sherry. 'I'm not going to look too far ahead.'

'Quite right, my dear. I see that van Diederijk hasn't altered anything—even the carpet in the hall.'

She sniffed. 'He told me I could have it mended…' she stopped and touched her companion's sleeve. 'Who on earth is that?' she asked.

Dr Bell followed her gaze. 'Ah, that is Diana Sibley, van Diederijk's fiancée.' He coughed. 'The daughter of a baronet.'

Euphemia took a good look without actually staring. 'She looks very conscious of the fact,' she said softly, disliking what she saw. Miss Sibley was tall and slender to the point of boniness, with no bosom worth mentioning and a long face and a straight nose above a thin-lipped mouth cleverly concealed by the masterly application of lipstick. Her eyes were dark, and as she came nearer Euphemia, still disliking her, decided that her dark hair owed more to a good hairdresser than to nature. She was beautifully dressed and she was smiling. Euphemia thought she was cold, as cold as Dr van Diederijk; if they had children, they would be a bunch of little icicles. She giggled into her sherry and earned a cold glance from her host, which emboldened her to grin at him and then turn her back. Dr Bell looked worried for a moment and then plunged into gentle conversation until she interrupted him with: 'I'm dreadfully sorry, that was awful of me—I hope she didn't see me, only I thought…'

She told him about the little icicles and went on fever-ishly: 'I'm talking nonsense—I shouldn't have come. I've not had anything to eat since midday and I thought it would be all right, but I can't forget…it takes a little while, doesn't it?'

The old man took her hand. 'My dear child, you were brave to come, your father would have been proud of you.' He patted her hand. 'He wouldn't want you to grieve, you know, he wasn't that kind of man.'

'No, I know, and I won't, only being here…' She glanced round the familiar room and caught the doctor's eye fastened upon her. He said something to his fiancée and came across the room before Euphemia could move, and Dr Bell said at once: 'Euphemia hasn't had anything to eat all day.'

Dr van Diederijk looked down his nose at her. 'That would explain it,' he said suavely. 'We will go to the kitchen and see what can be found.'

Euphemia went red. 'There's no need—I was going in a few minutes…'

'All the more reason to eat first.' He had ushered her to the door and out into the hall while he was speaking and she was in the kitchen before she could think of an answer.

Mrs Cross was standing at the table slicing ham, and she looked up and beamed at them both as they went in. 'There ain't no more of them canopies,' she observed, 'them waiters 'as taken the lot, but there's all them sausages.' She went back to her slicing. 'Nice ter see yer both together—both being owners of the 'ouse, like.'

Euphemia picked up a sausage. 'Dr van Diederijk rents this house, Mrs Cross. I still own it.' She bit into the sausage with something of a snap and added as an after-thought: 'No offence, Doctor.'

'Trivialities do not offend me, Miss Blackstock. Pray eat all you wish. You will excuse me if I go back to my guests.'

'Not only will I excuse you, Doctor, I don't really mind you going in the least.' Euphemia picked up another sausage.

'What an abominable girl you are!' The doctor spoke softly in a steely voice as he went away.

'You didn't ought ter, Miss Euphemia,' protested Mrs Cross. "'E might say 'e didn't want the 'ouse any more, and then where are yer?'

Euphemia selected a slice of ham, wrapped it round another sausage and gobbled it down. 'He signed a contract for a year.'

'Such a nice young man, too,' said Mrs Cross.

'He's not young, and he's certainly not nice.' Euphemia wandered out of the kitchen, taking an apple from a bowl on the table as she went.

She was sitting on the stairs munching it when the drawing room door opened and the doctor came out. He paused when he saw her, closed the door behind him and stood leaning against it, watching her.

'Eve and the apple,' he observed blandly.

'My name is Euphemia.' She nibbled at the core with splendid teeth.

'I was employing a figure of speech.'

'Oh, so who am I tempting?'

He said silkily: 'Not me, I do assure you, Euphemia. What an extraordinary name! Diana—my fiancée—would like to meet you.'

She got to her feet, the apple core still in her hand, very conscious of her bad manners earlier on. She said formally: 'That's very kind of her. Is she in the drawing-room?'

For answer he opened the door and she went past him. Diana Sibley was across the room, talking to Dr Bell, although her eyes were on the door. Half way there Euphemia remembered the apple core in her hand. She paused just long enough to hand it to the doctor before advancing, smiling nicely, to meet her.

CHAPTER THREE

DIANA SIBLEY had switched on her most charming smile, which was a pity, since it was quite wasted on Euphemia. 'Miss Blackstock, I've been dying to meet you—you're our guardian angel, you know, letting us have this darling house. I simply couldn't face the idea of living in an hotel every time Tane had to come to London.' She added carelessly, 'My parents' place is in Hertfordshire—there's room enough for us both to live there while we're in England, but Tane doesn't want to do that.' She gave him an arch look. 'He doesn't like the idea of sharing me with anyone, do you, darling?'

Euphemia was pleased to see that the doctor looked extremely uncomfortable and, behind his bland face, angry. She had no doubt that he was clenching his teeth in an effort not to tell his beloved to hush up. She said sweetly: 'I'm so glad you like the house. I'm sure you would rather be here with the doctor than with your family.'

Diana put a thin useless-looking hand on the doctor's sleeve. 'Not until we're married.' She made big eyes at them in turn. Dr van Diederijk richly deserved her, thought Euphemia as Diana went on: 'Tane wasn't going to ask you, but I insisted, and I so hoped you'd come. You're awfully brave, in your place I couldn't have done it.' She shuddered and gave Euphemia another smile, although her eyes were like dark pebbles and just as hard. 'I expect you're very strong, you must be to be a nurse.' She studied Euphemia smilingly with her head on one side. 'Anyone over eight stone seems huge to me,' she confided.

Euphemia's tawny eyes travelled slowly down Diana's spare frame. 'Not really,' she said cheerfully, 'just normal.' She saw the girl's mouth tighten with annoyance and added: 'So nice to have met you—and now I must just say hello to some of the people I know here.' She put out a hand. 'Thank you for asking me—I must go very soon, I'm on duty early in the morning.' She included the doctor in her smile, dropped a kiss on Dr Bell's cheek and crossed the room to join some friends. Diana, left alone with her fiancé, watched her, instantly surrounded by welcoming cries. 'Anyone would think she owned the place,' she declared thinly.

The doctor gave her a thoughtful look. 'But, my dear, she does,' he pointed out.

Euphemia left a few minutes later, seen politely to the door by her host. She uttered the usual banalities about a pleasant evening, how nice to meet his fiancée and she did hope that he would be happy there; she altered that to 'you both' in the same breath, then because he didn't say anything and she felt awkward standing there in the open doorway being stared at in such silence she went on: 'I expect you're looking for a house to suit you both for— later on when you're married...'

'You are free to expect anything you wish, Euphemia.'

She went past him and started down the drive to the gate, neatly mended now, she noticed. A great many things she would like to say to him were jostling for a place on her tongue, but she held it prudently. After all, she needed the rent money and the likelihood of seeing him again was remote.

Not remote at all. Sir Richard, doing his morning round on the following morning, brought Dr van Diederijk with him. The two gentlemen trod with deliberation into the ward, followed by the Medical Registrar, the House Physician, the Social Worker, a physiotherapist and a clutch of selfconscious students, and Euphemia, advancing to meet them with her staff nurse and one of the lesser fry clutching the patients' notes, came to a rather abrupt halt at the sight of him.

'You know each other, of course,' observed Sir Richard airily. 'Tenant and landlady, as it were, Sister. Dr van Diederijk has joined the consultant staff here, so you will see him from time to time, though not as often as we would wish for as he has commitments at St Chad's as well as Birmingham and Edinburgh, not to mention his appointments in Holland.'

Euphemia murmured suitably, cast a quick glance at the Dutchman and discovered him to be smiling faintly. It wasn't a very friendly smile, she decided; possibly he was amused at having taken her by surprise. She smiled in her turn in a wintry sort of way and then led on to the first bed.

It took her less than ten minutes to discover that Dr van Diederijk the doctor was somewhat different from the man. There was no sign of the cold arrogance or the bland mockery which she had encountered; he was calmly assured, ready to listen to the patients' sometimes rambling accounts of their illnesses, making no effort to steal Sir Richard's thunder, although it was obvious that he knew what he was about, making quiet, pertinent observations and questioning the students and getting far more answers than his colleague, who enjoyed a reputation for terrifying his students, anyway. He spoke seldom to her and then only to question treatment, addressing her in a cool, impersonal voice as though they had met for the first time. Standing patiently while the two men bent over the next patient, Mr Rumbold, admitted that morning with acute nephritis, she imagined him living at Myrtle House, sitting in the drawing-room, wandering round the garden, eating his solitary meals in the dining-room—not that he would be solitary for long once his Diana had got him to the altar. It was strange that they hadn't married. There was no reason why they shouldn't; he could support a wife in comfort, she imagined, and Diana had all the hallmarks of a girl who had led a leisured life with enough money to spend. The only reason she could think of was that they didn't really love one another enough to bother.

She was interrupted in these musings by Dr van Diederijk, asking her in a voice of exaggerated patience if he might have the X-rays of the patient he was examining. They were almost at the end of the round. Euphemia decided suddenly that she didn't want to have coffee with him and Sir Richard; she beckoned Staff Willis, whispered in her ear and led her party to the next and last bed.

Ten minutes later pouring her own coffee after serving the two men, she looked up with well simulated surprise as Willis knocked on the door of her office and asked if she could come into the ward.

'Anything urgent, Staff?' enquired Sir Richard.

Willis looked startled. A nice girl, but no imagination, thought Euphemia crossly. She said quickly before Willis could put her foot in it. 'I'll take a look, sir, and let you know.' She smiled at the two men and went to the door. Dr van Diederijk got to his feet as she edged past him. 'A pity, Sister,' he said pleasantly. 'I was hoping for a chance to renew our acquaintance—some other time, perhaps.'

She had no choice but to look at him. He was smiling his nasty little smile again, just as though he knew... She said snappily: 'Yes, of course, sir,' and swept out of the little room.

She stayed in the ward for five minutes and then went back to her office. If she remained away longer than that they might come to see what was keeping her. She had timed it very nicely; they were on the point of going. She assured them that the matter had been a trivial one and escorted them to the door, bidding them goodbye before nipping back into the office to drink her cooling coffee.

She went down to Middle Wallop for her next days off, driving the Morris after coming off duty in the early evening. It had been a warm day and the sky was hazy with a hint of thunder in the air. Once on the M3 she urged the Morris to its utmost speed, glad when she was past the turning she would have taken if she had been going home to Hampton-cum-Spyway. Lightning was streaking the sky as she switched to the A30 and she felt relief that another twenty miles or so would see her safely at her aunt's house. Once through Stockbridge she took the narrow road running alongside the river, going a good deal more slowly. The village was a fair size, set amongst rolling countryside. Euphemia turned away from its centre into a quiet lane behind the church and stopped outside a small house with plastered walls and a thatched roof. The thatch was in sad need of repair, but to a casual passer-by it was a charming place. Only Aunt Thea knew how awkward it was to run, with open fires and a temperamental boiler for the hot water and a leak in the roof when it rained too hard, but it had been her home all her married life and now that she was a widow, the idea of leaving it for something easier and modern never entered her head. She came to the door now, smiling and welcoming, and a moment later Ellen joined her. Euphemia, walking up the short path to meet them, was relieved to see how well her sister looked. This was the kind of life she should lead, obviously; she had always been a timid child and a shy young woman, but she looked relaxed and happy. Euphemia gave her a great hug and then kissed her aunt. 'How marvellous you both look,' she declared. 'I think I shall give up my job and rusticate.'

She had meant it as a joke, but Ellen said at once: 'Oh, I so wish you could, Phemie—it's such fun being here.' She added uncertainly: 'But of course you wouldn't, would you?'

'No, love, I like my job, you know.' She could have added that they would have all been in Queer Street if she gave it up, but she didn't; to have disturbed Ellen's newfound serenity would have been cruel.

It was over their late supper that Aunt Thea mentioned the new curate, nodding and smiling at Euphemia as she explained about Ellen doing the church flowers and helping with the village play-group. Euphemia, too prac-

tical to allow herself to daydream, nonetheless had an
instant mental picture of Ellen floating down the aisle on
the curate's arm. That sort of thing happened in novels, but
it would be nice, she thought, if it could happen just once
in real life for her sister. And for me too, she thought wist-
fully—to dismiss the idea at once. For the time being at
least, what she needed was money, not romance. It struck
her forcibly that by the time she had the finances straight
she would be looking middle age in the face and rather past
the romance bit. 'Oh, well,' she muttered, and sighed, so
that Aunt Thea wanted to know if she had a headache.

Her two days of freedom went too quickly, pottering
round the house, taking Gyp, her aunt's elderly spaniel, for
a sedate walk, going with Ellen to look at the church,
where they found the curate contemplating the west
window and obviously waiting for them. He seemed a nice
young man, rather quiet and solemn, but he had honest
blue eyes and a kind mouth and he was right for Ellen, that
was plain to Euphemia, and she only hoped that something
would come of it. Probably it would, she decided hopefully. Neither Ellen nor the curate were the type to fall in
love lightly. She had made some excuse to go on to the
village on a mythical errand and left them together.

London, when she reached it, was hot and humid and
teeming. She pushed the Morris doggedly through the
traffic, reached the hospital and parked in the yard at the
back. The car park for staff was full, as usual, so she would
have to come down later and move the car before she went
off duty that evening. She got out reluctantly, dragged her
overnight bag from the back seat and put it on the ground
while she wrestled with the car door. The lock jammed

from time to time, and it was jamming now; luckily she had time and to spare. She opened her bag and found a nail file and set to work on the lock's inside, poking and prodding with the expertise of long practice. She was halfway there when Dr van Diederijk's voice came from behind her.

'I won't offer to help,' he observed blandly, 'because I can see that you know exactly what you're about.' He added annoyingly: 'You need a new car.'

Euphemia gave him a fiery look. 'We're not all as rich...' she stopped abruptly: being rude wasn't going to help, and who knew, perhaps he might rent her home for another year.

'Just so, Euphemia.' He read her thoughts so unerringly that she went a guilty red and rammed the nail file into the lock so hard that it snapped in two. He took the pieces from her without a word, produced a penknife and finished the job for her. 'If not a new car, a new lock,' he suggested silkily.

'Thanks!' She banged the car door shut and turned away, to find him beside her. 'You had a pleasant time with your aunt?' he asked gently.

She gave him a surprised look. 'How did you know?...' she began.

'Oh, a chance remark from someone or other. Pretty country round the Wallops, although it's charming at Hampton-cum-Spyway. I'm very satisfied with your home, Euphemia.'

'I'm glad to hear it, Doctor. And now, if you don't mind, I haven't much time...'

He glanced at his watch. 'On duty at two o'clock?' he wanted to know. 'Half an hour for your meal, and that leaves almost an hour in which to change. You surprise me, you hadn't struck me as being one of those fussy young women who take hours to dress.'

'I don't think you meant that as a compliment,' she observed tartly, 'but even the plainest of us are improved with a little attention to detail.'

He smiled slowly. 'Now, when have I ever called you plain, Euphemia?'

He held open a side door for her and she skipped inside, annoyed that he was laughing at her, and she didn't reply to his quiet goodbye.

There were a number of really ill patients on the ward and she had little time to ruminate over her affairs. Once or twice she found herself thinking about Dr van Diederijk and his frightful fiancée. Miss Diana Sibley was like the Other Woman in a bad novel. Euphemia wondered what on earth had made him propose to her in the first place—certainly not her money, from all accounts he had more than enough of that, and although she was pretty in a washed-out sort of way, without her beautiful clothes and clever make-up she would be a very ordinary girl indeed.

Euphemia shook her head, lost in wonderment that a man with the good looks Dr van Diederijk had should fall for such a girl. 'Not that looks are anything to go by,' she told herself aloud. 'Look what a tiresome man he is behind that handsome face!' And then: 'And you can stop thinking about him, my girl, or you'll end up liking him after all!'

But there seemed no fear of that when he did his next round with sir Richard. His cold: 'Good morning, Sister,' followed by an absolute minimum of remarks addressed to herself, did nothing to make her like him any the better.

True, he joined in the small talk over their coffee in her office, but only when good manners made it necessary. Fortunately Sir Richard was in one of his more expansive moods and was happy enough to do most of the talking. Euphemia, put out by Dr van Diederijk's cool goodbyes at the ward door, kept her mouth firmly closed and did no more than nod her head in what she hoped was a gracious manner.

Despite that she felt a pang of pity for him later on in the day. She was crossing the entrance hall to see if there was any post for her when she glanced out of the long windows on each side of the door. Dr van Diederijk was standing outside talking to Diana Sibley. Euphemia, overcome by curiosity, paused to look. It was another warm day and Miss Sibley was dressed accordingly in a simple sheath of a dress which must have cost the earth, her feet were sandalled in rose pink leather and had ridiculous high heels and her hair looked as though she had come straight from the hairdressers. Euphemia allowed herself a few moments of envy before deciding that she would rather be her own slightly plump self than the fashionable vision leaning so gracefully against the white sports car which must be hers. She was on the point of turning away when Diana put out a hand and lifted a cheek which the doctor pecked with no enthusiasm at all. His kiss wasn't received with any degree of pleasure, either. Diana rubbed her cheek carefully, as though to rub it away, got into her car, blew a kiss at him, and drove away. He had his back to her now, and Euphemia wished that she could have seen his face, because somehow his broad back didn't look as though it belonged to a man in love. Granted, they couldn't have embraced fervently in full view of anyone

who chose to look from the hospital windows, but that
frigid peck need not have been quite so icy. Perhaps they
had quarrelled? Perhaps Diana didn't like to be kissed, or
to display her feelings in public? Euphemia, the post quite
forgotten, tried to decide, so deep in thought that she didn't
even notice the doctor come through the door, pause when
he saw her, then tread softly to her.

'Peeping Tom?' he enquired nastily.

Euphemia frowned and wished that she didn't blush so
easily. 'Certainly not,' she said coldly. 'I'm on my way to
collect the post—I was merely glancing out of the
window.'

'Haven't you got a young man?' he asked.

She glared at him. 'That's no business of yours, doctor!'

'I stand corrected; it's as well if we mind our own
business, don't you agree?' He strolled away before she
had an answer ready.

Euphemia fumed each time she thought about it, but
still, at the back of her head, was that little pang of pity
because his Diana had had no love in her face when she
had held it up for his kiss, no affection even, and yet she
had been so sickeningly coy at his party. She could have
puzzled about it all day, only she didn't have the time.

It was a week before she saw him again, a not very
happy week, for she had had a letter from the boys bemoaning the fact that they would have to spend their
holidays at Aunt Thea's and couldn't she do something
about it, and another one from Ellen asking if she could
possibly have some money to buy some new clothes. It was
a very gentle request and Euphemia knew that her sister
would accept a refusal without a murmur, all the same, she

would send something. Ellen had found herself a little job in the village, spending a few hours each day with an old lady who was almost blind and needed someone to read to her and do small jobs around the house, but she had only just started and she was to be paid monthly and the month still had almost its full length to go. Euphemia did some rather anxious sums on the household budget and wondered if she dared to send the boys to an old family friend in Scotland, who would love to have them, but there again, hadn't enough money to have them as guests—besides, there was the rail fare.

The ward wasn't easy either. She had never had to nurse so many cross old men, all demanding this, that and the other thing and driving her and the nurses to the point of screaming. Not that it showed. She went up and down the ward with a serene face, although it was difficult to keep it that way. As she pointed out to her staff nurse, if any of them had been really ill, she wouldn't have found it tiresome.

She was sitting at her desk writing up the Kardex during a lull in the evening's work when Dr van Diederijk, after the briefest of knocks, walked in. He wasted no time in pleasantries other than a brisk 'Good evening', and didn't wait for her to reply before observing: 'I hear that you have three weeks' holiday, Sister Blackstock?'

She crossed the T's and dotted the I's before she looked at him. 'Yes—why do you want to know?'

He looked at her thoughtfully. 'Been busy?' he asked smoothly. 'I understand that there are some tiresome patients on the ward. Your temper is short, perhaps?'

'Yes,' said Euphemia crossly, and bent her head to her Kardex, only to come upright in her chair at his next words.

'I have a favour to ask of you.' He had pulled up the only other chair in the little room and had seated himself opposite her.

She opened her eyes wide in astonishment. 'A favour? Me? I don't believe it!'

He ignored this. 'I should like you to accompany Diana to Jerez—in Spain, you know. She has had, most unfortunately, the mumps very severely and badly needs a complete rest. She has an aunt living there who will be delighted to have her, but she cannot undertake—er—companionship…'

'Why can't she go somewhere in England?' asked Euphemia.

'She is in low spirits, her illness has left her languid and out of sorts. She cannot bear to be seen by any of her friends until she has quite recovered; she needs…' he paused, looking at the wall above Euphemia's head.

She said tartly: 'Someone to brush her hair and rub in all the best creams and urge her to eat her food—she's far too thin anyway.'

He transferred his gaze to her face and said distantly: 'Diana is the ethereal type.'

'That's all very well, but see what happens when she gets a bit off colour—she loses pounds and looks like a matchstick.'

'What a very rude young woman you are, but I didn't come her to wrangle with you. If you will undertake to go with Diana for two weeks of your holiday I propose to vacate Myrtle House for a month so that your sister and brothers can spend their holidays in their own home.'

Euphemia put down her pen slowly. 'You mean that we can live there—you won't be there at all?'

'I shall be in Holland for some of the time, and probably I shall visit Diana's parents as well, and Sir Richard has offered to put me up while I am in London.'

'Well, that's very generous of you, but I'm not sure…'

'You will receive a salary, of course.' He got to his feet. 'Think it over and let me know. I daresay the boys would find it pleasant to be back there for their holidays.'

'Well, yes. As a matter of fact…' She just stopped herself in time from telling him her problems. 'When do you want to know?'

'I'm going to Women's Medical to see a patient. I'll call in on the way back. Fifteen minutes.'

'But that doesn't give me much time to think it over.'

'Just so.' He smiled faintly and went away.

It would have been wonderful if she could have refused. He was so obviously certain that she was going to do as he had asked—dangling her old house before her like a carrot in front of a donkey. But she couldn't indulge in that luxury, she would accept, although the idea of spending two weeks in Diana's company filled her with grave misgivings. On the other hand, the boys would be overjoyed, Ellen too, and the money would come in very useful.

She applied herself to the Kardex once more and he was back again, in exactly fifteen minutes, standing in the doorway, not saying a word.

'You knew I'd say yes,' she told him snappily.

He nodded. 'When are you free so that we may talk about it?' He put his hands in his pockets and leaned comfortably against the door jamb. 'This evening?'

Euphemia closed the Kardex and folded her hands upon it. 'If you like,' she said, politely now, because it wasn't much use being anything else. 'My holiday starts in a week's time.'

'I know—Diana should be fit to travel by then, so it should all fit in very nicely.' He turned away from the door. 'Would you be ready by half past seven? I'll be outside—we can have something to eat and discuss the details.'

He had gone before she had had time to do more than begin, 'Well…'

She was late off duty, but she still had plenty of time in which to shower and change. She put on a two-piece, printed in pale colours, and hoped that it would be suitable for wherever they were going. She hardly thought it would be a Macdonald's; on the other hand, he wasn't likely to take her to the Savoy.

She was wrong, for that was exactly where he drove her. He had been waiting when she got to the hospital entrance and after the briefest of greetings, had stuffed her into the front seat of the Bentley without waste of time, beyond telling her that he had booked a table he had nothing to say and neither had she; a poor start to an evening out she was already regretting.

She wasn't sure, thinking about it afterwards, when she had begun to enjoy herself; perhaps it was the excellent sherry she had had before they started their meal, perhaps it was the rich smoothness of the quenelles of crawfish with lobster sauce and the excellent hock, followed by spiced chicken with apricots. Euphemia found herself liking her companion more and more; but it wasn't until they had eaten the sherry trifle and she had poured their coffee that the doctor mentioned her forthcoming journey.

They were to fly from Heathrow, she was told with a somewhat abrupt change of manner from the charm and friendliness to cool directions. He would drive his Diana there and Euphemia would meet them at a spot to be decided upon later. She would be kind enough to take good care of Diana on the journey, as she was still—er—frail. Her activities once she was safely at her aunt's house were to be limited to her wishes.

'And how do we get to her aunt's house?' enquired Euphemia.

'You will be met at the airport and driven there. The car will be at your disposal during your stay. I doubt if Diana will feel up to much exercise.' Which remark led Euphemia to ask naughtily:

'You did say mumps?'

His blue eyes became glacial. 'I must ask you not to joke about it, Euphemia. Diana has suffered a good deal, mentally as well as physically.'

'Why?'

He frowned at her. 'If it were not that I had such a splendid report of you from Sir Charles, I might reconsider my offer,' he said austerely.

Euphemia put down her coffee cup. 'And I might reconsider my acceptance…'

The smile she didn't like came and went. 'How disappointed your brothers will be! I take it that you have already told them?'

She stared at him across the table, her tawny eyes glowing with annoyance. 'Yes, I have.'

'Then shall we cry truce? I was beginning to think that we were establishing a pleasant relationship.'

'I can't imagine… Your Diana—does she want me to go with her?'

'She will be grateful for your help and support.'

Euphemia suppressed a giggle and at the severe glance, said: 'Sorry, only you make her sound like an infirm old lady.'

'Diana is twenty-eight and extremely active.'

'I'm twenty-seven.'

'More coffee?' She asked sweetly, 'And don't you know that it's frightfully rude to comment upon a woman's age?'

'But I am rude. You have never ceased to make me aware of this since we met.'

'Oh—I didn't mean…well, that's not quite true.'

'You don't need to make excuses, we can't all like each other.'

Euphemia said slowly: 'No,' and wondered why it was that she had been enjoying his company so much. He'd been putting himself out, of course, making himself pleasant deliberately, making sure that she would go with his beastly Diana. The thought made her feel sad.

'I'd better get back,' she told him, 'I'm on duty at eight o'clock. I think I've got your instructions right and I'll be at Heathrow wherever you want to meet me.'

'I'll let you know. Let me see, it's five days before your holiday, isn't it? You have a passport? Clothes? I'll contact you in two days' time. When does your holiday start?'

'In two days' time,' she said flatly.

He only nodded and said nothing, and presently he drove her back, making conversation during the short drive to the hospital and not saying another word about his plans. Euphemia wished him a quiet good night at the entrance of the Nurses' Home and thanked him for her pleasant evening. It was disconcerting to be told coolly that he, for his part, had found only part of the evening pleasant.

He came into her office during the evening before she was due to go on holiday. 'You're going to your aunt's?' he asked after a brief 'Good evening'.

She looked her surprise. 'Yes, as a matter of fact, I am. Shall I give you her phone number?'

'If you wish I'll drive you down.'

'That wouldn't do. How do I get up to Heathrow?'

'Diana's father can drive her over there and I'll run you up.'

Euphemia put down her pen. 'That would never do and you know it!'

He considered this for a moment. 'Perhaps you're right. In that case I'll drive your car down and come back by train.'

'It's a frightful journey from Middle Wallop.'

He gave her a cool look. 'Trying to frighten me, Euphemia? You will be good enough to let me drive you down in your car, we can finalise the arrangements at our leisure. When do the boys come on holiday?'

'The day after tomorrow.'

'Good—Ellen will return at the same time? If not will the boys be all right on their own for a night?'

'Oh, yes, I've already written to Mrs Cross.' She hesitated. 'You're sure you don't mind?—us living there?'

'If I had minded I wouldn't have suggested it in the first place,' he said dampeningly.

'Oh, well. It's very kind of you—they'll all love it. We'll leave it exactly as you wish when we go.' She smiled suddenly. 'I'll have a few days there when I come back from Jerez.'

'So I imagined. At what time do you intend to leave here?'

'About ten o'clock, the early morning traffic won't be so fierce by then.'

His lips twitched. 'I shall be driving,' he reminded her.

'But it's my car and the only car I've got.'

He laughed and looked years younger. 'I promise you I'll be careful.'

'All right, then, nine o'clock if you'd rather.'

'Shall we meet by your car, then?' He smiled briefly and went away, and Euphemia, being a sensible girl with a lot of work to do, dismissed him from her mind and got on with it.

CHAPTER FOUR

HE WAS THERE by her car when she reached it, immaculate in tweeds and a thin polo-necked sweater. His good morning was friendly and he waited patiently as she unlocked the car door. 'There's time to call in at Myrtle House,' he suggested. 'Mrs Cross said she would be there.'

Euphemia hadn't expected that. 'You're very kind,' she said, 'that would be nice,' and settled herself into the seat beside his, hoping rather naughtily that the car would play up as it so often did with her. But it didn't. They wound their way through the morning traffic and reached Myrtle House without single mishap, and she spent half an hour giving Mrs Cross instructions as to what to do when the boys and Ellen arrived. They had coffee in the sitting room and the doctor was a nice blend of host and guest. Euphemia wasn't quite sure what she was.

They reached Middle Wallop in time for a late lunch, and Aunt Thea, warned in advance by telephone, had done them proud. She was an excellent cook and after the first little flurry of introductions and small talk over a glass of very sweet sherry which Euphemia guessed the doctor didn't much care for, she sent them into the small dining room. There was watercress soup, followed by pasties and a salad, very different from the salads served at the hospital—a lettuce leaf and a sliver of tomato and if you were lucky, slice of cucumber. Aunt Thea's salads were a dream: mint and chives and lettuce from the garden, tomatoes from the greenhouse, tiny spring onions, cucumber cubes and baby beetroots, all bathed in a dressing of her own invention. Euphemia was surprised to see the doctor tucking in with genuine pleasure and when Aunt Thea darted into her kitchen and came back with a bowl of raspberries and dish of thick cream he observed: 'I can't remember when I have enjoyed a meal as much, Mrs Cooper,' at which Aunt Thea smiled widely.

'Well, it's a pleasure to cook for guests; since my husband died, there's not much incentive to plan a meal.'

The doctor questioned her gently and she responded, glad to talk about the late Colonel Cooper. Euphemia, watching her aunt's rather shy manner warm under his interest, decided that he was adept worming his way into someone else's graces. But he'd better not try that with me, she thought, the wily old devil—and then amended the thought honestly. Not a devil and not wily and certainly not old; arrogant and a great one for wanting his own way and getting it too, and his cool way of snubbing her left much to be desired. She wondered uneasily if there was another side to him which she hadn't been allowed to see. Probably his Diana saw him in a quite different light. She munched raspberries and speculated on this, and then looking up caught his eye and pinkened a little because she had the nasty feeling that he knew exactly what she was thinking.

Ellen offered to take him to the church after lunch which surprised Euphemia very much, as Ellen was shy of strangers, but the doctor had a way with him there was no denying that. She watched her sister going down the garden path chattering away as though she had known the doctor all her life, and then went into the kitchen to help with the washing up, feeling hard done by.

The two of them came back more than an hour later, but this time they were accompanied by the curate, on excellent terms with the doctor and only too ready to stay for what Aunt Thea called a cup of tea but which turned out to be accompanied by paper-thin cucumber sandwiches, fairy cakes and a nice old-fashioned fruit cake, demolished to the last crumb by her guests.

The two men left together, the curate to accompany the doctor to the station half a mile away. Dr van Diederijk took a warm farewell of his hostess and Ellen, a somewhat cooler one of Euphemia, with the reminder that she was to be at Heathrow Airport on the morning of the day after tomorrow at ten o'clock precisely, bearing her passport and such money as she thought necessary. The tickets had already been arranged for, and he reminded her also to have as little luggage as possible. He had said all this on their way down, but she nodded politely and wished him goodbye and didn't linger in the doorway to see him go.

The curate drove her up to Heathrow in her own car with Ellen for company and the promise to come and collect her on her return. It was a lovely morning and still early. Euphemia sat back, watching the country in the height of its summer glory, and wondering if she had been a little mad. She had never fancied Spain and she certainly didn't fancy Diana Sibley; on the other hand Myrtle House would be home for all of them for one glorious month. Not for her, of course, but there would be almost a week left when she got back from Jerez-something to look forward to.

They arrived in good time at Heathrow and she had expected to wait. Dr van Diederijk, elegant in summer suiting, dispelled the faint panic she had felt as she got out of the car. She wasn't sure where he had come from, but there he was, looking calm, very much at ease and dealing with her case and ticket with the air of a man who had done it all before. Probably he had, dozens of times, she told herself as she followed him into the reception hall after goodbyes had been said.

'Diana is upstairs in the lounge,' he told her. 'She feels a little under the weather.'

Which was probably why she was wearing a gossamer scarf over her head and draped across the lower half of her face. Euphemia, bareheaded and cool in a short-sleeved shirtwaister, by no means new but elegant and entirely suitable for the journey, surveyed the other girl's flowing draperies and wondered why on earth she should choose to wear something so awkward for a plane journey.

'So there you are,' observed Diana waspishly. 'If we have to sit here much longer I shall be ill. Do something about it, Tane!'

'Not possible, Diana, I'm afraid,' said the doctor soothingly, 'but your flight should be called at any moment now and you should be comfortable enough once you're on board. In a few hours you will be at your aunt's house and able to relax.'

Diana could have been smiling, it was impossible to

tell with all that veiling, but her eyes, heavily made up, opened wide and she flicked the lashes at him. 'Dear Tane,' she said in her well modulated voice, 'so thoughtful—I shall miss you.'

'And I you, but this holiday will restore you to your old self again.' A voice bade them go to the gate and join their flight and Euphemia got to her feet composedly, picked up her shoulder bag, accepted Diana's enormous crocodile one, and followed the two of them down the stairs to the barrier where the doctor bade them a courteous goodbye without so much as taking his fiancée's hand in his. And that wouldn't do for me, decided Euphemia silently, as she shepherded her charge through Customs.

Once on board, ensconced in comfort in the first class section, Diana signified her intention of having a nap. 'And I don't want to be disturbed,' she added sharply. She pulled off her veil then, revealing an unhealthily pale face, far too thin, lines of discontent deeply scored between mouth and nose. 'Look at me,' she declared bitterly, 'I've always been beautiful, everyone says so, and now I'm as plain as any other girl.'

Euphemia allowed her calm professional mask to hide her feelings. 'That's because you need to get out into the sun and air—I daresay you've been indoors all day…'

'Well, of course I have—I'm far too delicate to go racketing around when I've been so ill. I'm not a great tough creature like you, I'm sensitive, I always have been, but I manage to hide it—even Tane was surprised to see how badly the mumps affected me. It was he who insisted on this holiday.' She gave a self-satisfied little laugh. 'He's so careful of me; I'm to lie in the garden and swim each day and eat anything I fancy. He insisted on you coming with me, too.' She added patronisingly: 'He seems to think you're a good nurse, and of course, only the very best is good enough for me.'

Euphemia had nothing to say to this—indeed, she didn't think that Diana expected a reply, anyway. She made her comfortable and then sat back in her seat, accepted a cold drink from the stewardess and looked out of the window. They were over water and there was land ahead. England had been left behind already.

She had been looking forward to the flight. Looking down on other countries was a new experience for her, but her thoughts became more and more engrossing, so that presently she had no idea where they were and didn't much care. Diana Sibley was a horrid young woman, conceited, spoilt and selfish. Why on earth Dr van Diederijk wanted to marry her was beyond Euphemia's comprehension; she had never once seen even the faintest spark of feeling between the two of them, although she had to admit that they could possibly be so reserved that they kept their feelings hidden in public. She frowned. The first time she had met Diana she had been nauseatingly coy and posses- sive towards the doctor, although his manner towards her had been pleasant and nothing else. She would really have to find out… Perhaps he had been tricked into an engage- ment? Unlikely considering the kind of man he was. Perhaps he had had his heart broken and didn't care whom he married? Euphemia pursued this idea in some depth until she became quite carried away and actually felt sorry for him. He needed rescuing before he found himself tied up for the rest of his life to Diana. Perhaps he wasn't such a bad man after all, thought Euphemia on a wave of sympathy, and he had been very kind about Myrtle House…perhaps she could find a way of helping him out of an awkward situation.

They were met at Seville Airport by a uniformed chauffeur, who ushered them into an immense Cadillac with an air of reverence and saw to all the tiresome details of luggage and tipping. Euphemia, sitting back in her corner, heaved a sigh of relief; Diana had wakened in a frightful temper and it had been no easy matter to get her off the plane and through Customs without setting everyone's teeth on edge. She sat beside her now, the veil discarded because, as she pointed out crossly, none of her friends were within hundreds of miles to stare at her spoiled looks, grumbling at the heat, the slowness of the porters, the journey ahead of them… How could anyone, let alone Dr van Diederijk, love such an ill-tempered creature? All the same, Euphemia reminded herself, she had promised to look after Diana and get her back to her normal self again, and she had no intention of backing out of that promise.

The chauffeur got into the car, urged it through the traffic and joined the motorway south, bypassing Utrero and disappointingly cutting out a number of villages and small towns Euphemia would have liked to see. She was a little disappointed in the scenery around her, but she told herself sensibly that away from the main roads it was probably quite different. Now all she could see as they tore along was a seemingly unending plain with few trees and those small and umbrella-shaped, the olive groves giving way to row upon row of vines; bleak even in the bright sun but impressive too.

But she had second thoughts as they approached Jerez; it was a much larger place than she had thought and it looked interesting, but before she could see much of it the chauffeur turned the car off the main road and drove along a narrow, ill-surfaced road which took them through the outskirts to slightly higher ground. Presently there were high iron railings on one side and then a closed gate which was opened as the chauffeur sounded his horn and started up a broad drive, beautifully kept and bordered on either side by palm trees, jacaranda trees and great splashes of bougainvillea as the drive wound round a corner and the house came into view. Euphemia could see roses, crimson and yellow and pink climbing over its white walls. The house was large and low and beautiful; even without its magnificent grounds it would have been that. Euphemia forgot her first disappointment. This was Spain as she had imagined it, and she sighed with pleasure as they got out of the car. The door was open and an elderly woman dressed in black was standing there to welcome them—not Mrs Kellard of course, the housekeeper probably, smiling and wishing them good day in sparse English. Euphemia returned the greeting, but Diana swept inside with an impatient: 'Where is my aunt?'

They were conducted across a vast cool hall and into an equally vast room, its french windows open to the gardens beyond. It was furnished in the Spanish style, dark wood, heavily carved, and there was a profusion of flowers. Diana's aunt was reclining on a chaise-longue, swathed in gossamer draperies, and made no attempt to get up as they entered. She was an older edition of her niece, a thin, faded lady with an acidulated face and an elaborate

hair-style, and her voice, small and rather shrill, was as
faded. 'There you are, Diana—and you've brought your
nurse with you? A good thing, because I'm quite unable
to undertake any arduous tasks at the moment—this
heat…'

Diana crossed the room and kissed her aunt an inch
away from her cheek and said shortly: 'Yes, here's the
nurse. Her name's Euphemia.'

'Extraordinary!' Mrs Kellard lifted her head a couple
of inches the better to look at Euphemia, who stayed where
she was, and stared coolly back. Somehow she had
imagined the aunt to be a perfectly normal person, and here
she was, a second Diana, only more so. Euphemia sighed
to herself and said in voice of great politeness: 'How do
you do, Mrs Kellard.'

Mrs Kellard looked taken aback, just as though she
hadn't expected to be spoken to by a nurse, then said
grudgingly: 'I hope you will be happy here, Nurse…'

'Blackstock.'

'Blackstock—er—my poor niece has been very ill, so
I'm told, and I'm sure she will need your services.' She
added: 'You are a trained nurse, I hope?'

'I'm a Ward Sister, Mrs Kellard, and I've come as
Diana's companion to oblige Dr van Diederijk.'

Mrs Kellard said faintly: 'Oh, well, of course…you two
girls can make your arrangements, just let Maria know.
Diana, ring the bell, please, you'll want to go to your
rooms and rest. Have tea sent up if you want to—I'll see
you both at dinner.'

Diana had a huge room opening on to a balcony overlooking the gardens at the front of the house. Euphemia

saw her safely into it with a promise to return very shortly, and followed her guide down the wide corridor to a similar room on the other side of the house. It was smaller but just as comfortably furnished, with its own small balcony and bathroom. Euphemia took a quick satisfied look and went back to Diana.

She found her on the bed complaining that she was exhausted, while a maid unpacked her cases. Euphemia said with mild authority: 'A cool bath will do you good, then a cup of tea and a rest in bed until it's time to change for the evening.'

'I'm too tired…'

'Dr van Diederijk would like to see you well again as quickly as possible, so shall we start right away? Two weeks isn't too long. We shall have to plan some kind of programme, I think…'

'Why?' Diana asked peevishly. 'I don't feel like doing anything, and I don't see why I should.' She added with a faint whine: 'I've been ill.'

'Mumps,' observed Euphemia levelly. 'Thousands of people have them every day of the year, now all you have to do is to be quick and get pretty again. You surely don't want to walk around with a veil over your face for ever?' She walked through to the bathroom, saying over her shoulder, 'Dr van Diederijk will be so pleased to find you your old self again.'

She took a couple of towels from the pile laid ready and set them handily for the shower. Would he be pleased? she wondered, and then dismissed the thought as a mean one.

Dinner, taken in a high-ceilinged room opening on to the garden, was a serious affair. Euphemia was secretly thankful that she had packed one or two pretty summer dresses suitable for the evening, for both Mrs Kellard and Diana had changed into elaborate chiffon creations and while neither of them had said anything, she was only too well aware that they thought nothing of her pale patterned cotton voile. The meal itself was lengthy and over-elaborate, and since neither of the ladies ate more than a mouthful of each course, Euphemia was forced to curb her own healthy appetite. It was quite a relief when Diana said that she would go to bed immediately after their coffee and plainly expected Euphemia to go with her. Her aunt bade them good night, told them to ring for anything they might want, and picked up her book. She might have invited her niece to stay as a guest, but she seemed to have no idea about entertaining her.

In her room Diana undressed slowly, grumbling that she was exhausted and that her head ached.

'Well, I daresay it does,' observed Euphemia matter-of-factly. 'It's been a long day. Sit down and I'll brush your hair for you—and supposing you take a sleeping pill? Do you want anything in the morning or do you breakfast in bed?'

'I never get up for breakfast!' Diana sounded quite horrified. 'Don't come near me until ten o'clock. I want you to massage some of that cream on the dressing table into my neck and shoulders, and there's a mask for my face…'

It was more than an hour later that Euphemia got to her own room. She got ready for bed slowly, tired and dispirited. She was to be nothing more than a lady's maid to Diana, and the thought of a whole two weeks fetching and carrying for that young lady appalled her; only the knowledge that at the end of those two weeks she would be free to spend the rest of her holiday at Myrtle House with the boys and Ellen stopped her from bursting into quite unaccountable tears. She got into bed and lay between the cool sheets and thought about Dr van Diederijk. Somehow— she wasn't sure why—he seemed to be the main cause of her unhappiness.

But it was impossible to be unhappy when she wakened in the morning. The sun was up in a cloudless sky and it was already warm even at that early hour. She got up and showered and put on a sleeveless cotton dress, then went quickly through the house, intent on a cup of tea if it was to be had and then a stroll in the gardens. She met the house-keeper in the hall and was greeted with a look of such surprise that she asked what was the matter.

'You are up early, miss—the ladies do not usually appear before ten or eleven o'clock. You would like breakfast?'

Euphemia smiled at her, 'Yes, please. Where do I go?'

'The garden, perhaps? Coffee and rolls? They will be brought to you.'

It was glorious sitting in the sunshine on the broad patio. Euphemia gobbled up the rolls, drank all the coffee and started off for her walk. The garden was a large one and beyond it were shrubs and trees screening the house from the road beyond. She found a swimming pool almost at once, then wandered off down flower-bordered paths, going slightly uphill so that presently when she stopped and looked behind her, she could see a good deal of Jerez below her and the broad sweep of the land behind the town. In the morning sunlight it looked beautiful, quite unlike her first impression of it, perhaps because then she had seen it in the glare of the afternoon sun. Presently she strolled back to the house, pausing on the way to ask if she might have breakfast out of doors each morning, and enquiring where she might sit quietly and write some letters.

She was shown a small room, its walls lined with books behind glass-fronted cases and, she suspected, seldom read. But there was a comfortable desk under the window and a plentiful supply of notepaper. She spent the next hour or so happily writing to her family.

Diana greeted her petulantly. She declared that she hadn't slept at all, that she felt ill, that her eyes hurt her and she had no appetite for breakfast. 'I suppose you slept like a log,' she observed crossly, 'you're such a great healthy creature.'

Euphemia held her tongue. There was no point in annoying Diana still further. She was a bad-tempered girl, given to self-pity, although probably the doctor hadn't discovered that yet. She coaxed Diana from her bed, massaged her neck to dispel another headache, ran her bath and then brushed her hair. The mumps had caused it to fall out here and there and without its regular tinting it was returning to its normal brown; besides, it looked dull and lifeless. It was surprising what a good brushing did for it, though. Dressed and carefully made up, Diana looked a good deal better and in consequence consented to walk in the garden for a little while. The rest of the morning she spent on a chaise-longue, a big-brimmed hat protecting her pallid face from the sun and oiling herself with sun lotion, and Euphemia perforce sat beside her, a cotton sun-hat perched carelessly on top of her gleaming dark hair and not bothering about lotions, listening to her companion's endless chatter about herself, her clothes, and the number of friends she had, none of whom, it seemed, she liked. 'I've always been popular,' she informed Euphemia smugly, 'especially with men—I've had simply loads of them wanting to marry me. I don't suppose you've had a proposal, have you?'

'No,' said Euphemia goodnaturedly, feeling sorry for the girl even while she disliked her; how awful to be so wrapped up in herself. 'How did you meet Dr van Diederijk?' she asked.

Diana smirked. 'At a friend's house—oh, almost a year ago, and we became engaged six months later, I'm precisely the wife Tane wants, of course I understand the running of a large house and I'm a good hostess.' Her dark spiteful gaze rested for a moment on Euphemia's C & A cotton dress and the sun-hat, perched so carelessly. 'I know how to dress too.'

Euphemia, aware of the look, thought she would know how to dress too if she could have a purse as deep as Diana's, but she refrained from saying so and listened with astonishment and disgust to Diana's: 'I don't intend to have a child, but Tane's got so many brothers and sisters I can't see that it would matter. I mean, his name can be carried on by any of their children.'

Euphemia was glad that she was wearing her dark glasses. She said evenly: 'I should think that being married without having children was like eating beef without mustard.'

'What an extraordinary thing to say! I'm far too delicate in the first place, and I don't care for children—I have no doubt Tane will understand and agree with me—he has only just begun to realise how frail I am.'

Euphemia turned a snort into a cough. 'How fortunate that you're marrying a doctor,' and then suddenly sick of the conversation: 'How about a gentle swim in the pool— it's very good for getting you back into shape.'

'There's nothing wrong with my shape—I'm a little slimmer than usual, that's all.' Diana glanced town at her beanpole figure with complacency. 'But you may be right—it's a pity you don't know anything about massage.'

'Yes, isn't it.' Euphemia made her voice sound casually friendly. 'But there's no reason why you shouldn't get someone from Jerez to come up here.'

They spent ten minutes or so in the pool while Diana swam languidly up and down and then declared herself exhausted again. 'And you'd better come with me,' she declared. 'I feel quite faint.'

Euphemia muttered under her breath. Diana was a hypochondriac and getting worse with every passing hour— Tane van Diederijk must love her very much.

He telephoned after lunch that day, and Diana took the call and went straight to her room afterwards, while Euphemia wandered off into the shady corners of the garden once more and wondered what he had said.

The days passed slowly. It was soon obvious that Diana and her aunt did not intend to leave the house or the garden; the pair of them lay about, complaining of the heat. Indeed, Euphemia saw very little of Mrs Kellard, for apart from the elaborate dinner each evening, she remained on one chaise-longue or other, reading or telephoning her friends. The idea of entertaining her niece hadn't entered her head, and when Euphemia mildly suggested that they might take a drive in the cool of the late afternoon or go into Jerez in the early morning and see something of the town, she met with no success at all. 'Though I suppose if you want to go, there's nothing to stop you,' said Diana ungraciously. 'Tane said something about you having some time to yourself, but you don't do anything all day, do you?'

Euphemia didn't answer that. She was hardly over-worked, but the hair brushing, rubbing in of lotions and creams, the fetching and carrying and coaxing to get up in the morning, to eat, to sleep, to take exercise, to swim—her day wasn't her own; certainly the only time she felt quite free was in the morning before everyone else was up.

'I should like that,' she said pleasantly. 'I'll go when you're settled in the garden tomorrow morning.'

Diana looked surprised. 'Oh, all right, if you must—I daresay I'll find some shopping for you to do.' She added sharply: 'I don't suppose Aunt will let you have the car.'

'I don't want it, thank you. I shall enjoy the walk.'

At dinner that evening Euphemia was told that she was foolish to walk into Jerez. 'It's two miles at least and the road's bad,' said Mrs Kellard. 'I should have thought that a nurse would have more sense.'

Euphemia just smiled and said nothing. She never talked much at meals; for one thing, she wasn't often ad-dressed by her companions, and for another she needed as much time as possible to eat enough to keep her going while they pecked at their food.

Euphemia had made friends with the housekeeper and the gardener and was on nodding terms with the maids. They had told her where to go in Jerez and pointed out that there was a bus where the lane from the house joined the main road; it ran infrequently, but she might find it useful on the return journey. And she got away more quickly than she had hoped. Diana wanted quite a long list of things, so many in fact that Euphemia said that she might not get back in time for lunch.

'Well, that's your worry,' said Diana rudely. 'The servants don't do anything between half past one and four o'clock—you'll have to eat out, though I don't suppose it would hurt you to miss a meal.'

Euphemia's tawny eyes sparkled with rage. She said sweetly: 'I expect it's the mumps which has left you so irritable. Perhaps we should get a doctor...'

She whisked out of the room and out of the house and instantly felt better—after all, there were only eight days left of Diana's company, it was a heavenly morning, and she was free to potter round Jerez. She would be there in half an hour or so.

Only she wasn't. She had reached the narrow side gate Maria had told her would be a short cut when she heard a child crying. There was no one in the garden. Euphemia opened the gate and peered around her; the crying was faint and disjointed and it took her a few moments to locate its source—a small boy lying by the side of the lane. He was extremely dirty and wearing a torn T-shirt and brief, ragged trousers; moreover his face was bloodstained, as were his hands.

Euphemia hurried smartly across the lane and knelt beside him. The blood was from a nasty scalp wound and had partly dried, making his dirty face and hands even worse than they were, and his small monkey face was screwed up with fright and pain. Euphemia took her handkerchief and wiped his tears away and said, 'There, there, you'll soon be better.' He stopped his sobs for a moment to break into a torrent of Spanish. She couldn't understand a word, but she cuddled him close and after a few minutes he stopped crying and let her look at his head.

It was a nasty jagged cut which had bled a lot and since he had touched it with his hands heaven only knew if it was infected or not. She smiled reassuringly at him and noticed that his pupils were unequal, a sign that there was some local brain damage, she hoped nothing serious. But now she had to get help for him without delay, and luckily the house was only a couple of minutes' walk away; she would carry him there, put him to rest somewhere quiet, clean him up and get someone to telephone the doctor. He was only a little boy and she guessed not over-nourished, and it was easy enough to carry him up to the house. The front door stood open and it was the nearest. She made for it and had a foot inside the house when Mrs Kellard, coming slowly down the stairs, saw her and let out a shriek.

'It's all right,' said Euphemia soothingly, 'I found this child just outside the gate, he's been injured. If I could put him on a bed while someone telephones the doctor…'

Mrs Kellard seemed to swell with her indignation. 'You must be mad! Bring a filthy brat into my house—heaven knows what dirt and disease he'll bring with him. Don't come a step nearer!'

'Then may I take him to the servants' entrance?' Euphemia looked down at the small face against her shoulder. The child was only semi-conscious and needed help quickly. She looked up and saw Diana hanging over the banisters. 'Diana, this poor child is injured, will you help me?'

'Certainly not—God knows where he's from. They're

tough, these peasants, he'll get over it if you put him by the side of the lane—anyhow, someone will find him.'

Euphemia felt sick with horror. 'But you must!' she reiterated. 'His mother…'

'Won't have missed him,' interposed Mrs Kellard crisply. 'They have so many children they wouldn't even notice.'

Euphemia turned on her heel. There was a good deal she intended to say, but that would have to come later. First get help for the child. If she had known how to telephone she would have done so, but she didn't; the best thing was to carry the child down the lane to the main road and get help there. She started off down the drive, aware now that the child, light though he was, was getting heavier every minute. She was round the bend out of sight of the house when she heard a car coming, a shabby taxi, chugging up along the incline. She shouted 'Stop!' as it hove in sight, but there had been no need for that; it had already done so with a fine squealing of brakes. Its door opened and Dr van Diederijk jumped out.

CHAPTER FIVE

THE DOCTOR took the child from her and laid him gently on a grassy patch between the shrubs. 'Surely you would do better to go to the house?' he suggested without bothering to greet her.

'Don't be silly,' said Euphemia furiously. 'I've already been there. They—Mrs Kellard—wouldn't let me go in with him. He's dirty, you see.' The scorn in her voice caused the doctor to give her a searching look through narrowed eyes. 'I was taking him down to the main road— I thought I'd get a lift into Jerez, to the hospital—there must be one…' She put a gentle hand on the matted hair. 'He's concussed—he was conscious when I found him, about ten minutes ago.'

The doctor didn't look at her, he was examining the little boy with careful hands. 'That's a nasty wound, but I can't feel a fracture. We'll get him to the hospital at once.' He turned his head and said something to the driver in Spanish and the man, who had got out to look too, got back in and turned the car.

'You first, in the back,' said the doctor, and put the child on her knee and got in beside her, steadying the boy's head with firm hands. 'Well, tell me what happened,' he said. 'Just the facts, no personal comments.'

Euphemia went very red and then white. If she had had a free hand she would have hit him. She said in a wooden voice: 'I found him by the side of the lane outside the wicket gate at the top of the garden. I heard him crying. I can't understand Spanish, so I took a quick look at him and then carried him up to the house…'

'Go on.'

'There's no more to say.'

'Oh yes, there is—Mrs Kellard wouldn't allow you in. Why didn't you fetch Diana? You could at least have asked her to telephone.' He sighed. 'It was really rather silly of you to start traipsing off in this heat.' And when she didn't answer, 'Well?'

'You asked for the facts. I've given them.' Euphemia didn't look at him but stared out of the window at the beginnings of Jerez, her arms cradling the child. There really was no point in saying anything more. He wouldn't believe her, and it didn't matter in the least, anyway.

They didn't speak again until the taxi drew up with an exaggerated care engendered by the doctor's warning to the driver. The hospital looked modern; she had a brief glimpse of it as the doctor got out and took the boy from her. 'Stay here,' he ordered, and then paused at her: 'I have some shopping to do for Diana. I'll find my own way back.'

His cool blue eyes studied her from her head to her heels. 'My dear girl, have you looked at yourself lately?'

She was covered in dirt and bloodstains and somewhere along the way she had lost her sun-hat. 'You'll stay just

where you are, Euphemia,' said the doctor, 'and don't
waste my time arguing about it.'

A remark hardly calculated to put her in a good mood.
She opened the shoulder bag she still had with her and tried
to tidy herself under the amused eye of the driver. She
wasn't very successful—besides, it was hot in the taxi, the
street they were in was narrow, crowded with traffic and
people, although at its end she glimpsed a broad thorough-
fare lined with palm trees. She sat back and closed her
eyes; she had missed her chance of seeing something of
the town and perhaps she wouldn't get another one. Her
dress was ruined too… She opened her eyes at the sound
of voices and saw the doctor and a man in a long white coat
standing by the taxi. When the doctor turned his head
suddenly and looked at her she closed her eyes again, but
it was too late, the door was opened and she had to sit up
straight and be introduced to the other man, one of the
surgeons at the hospital. He was flatteringly interested in
her. How long had she been in Jerez? What did she think
of it? How long did she intend staying? She answered his
questions composedly and when he suggested that she
might like to see the hospital before she left, she agreed
pleasantly. 'But I would like to know how the little boy is.'

'A concussion and a cut head. We have asked the police
to trace his parents. Be assured that all will be done for his
comfort.' He was a good-looking man in a dark way, and
he smiled at her now. 'I cannot think how it is that I have
not met you sooner. You are so beautiful—Miss
Blackstock.'

She shot a sideways look at Dr van Diederijk standing
silently beside his companion, his face inscrutable. She

said clearly: 'Thank you, Doctor. My day hasn't been very pleasant so far, but I feel much better now, even though I don't believe you. Look at me!'

'But I have been looking at you, and you are beautiful.'

She gave him a very sweet smile. 'You are very kind. I hope we meet again.'

She shook hands and sat quietly while the two men said goodbye. The doctor got in presently and the taxi went on down the street and turned into the boulevard.

The doctor said tightly: 'There was no need to be quite so forthcoming, Euphemia.'

She turned to look at him, letting her thick lashes sweep her cheek and then lift to fringe wide eyes. 'What do you mean?' she asked sweetly.

'Don't provoke me, you know very well what I mean.' She decided that his smile wasn't very nice. 'Tell me about Diana—is there any improvement?'

Euphemia hadn't liked the smile. She lifted a nicely kept hand and ticked off her fingers one by one. 'Her hair is better—I brush it and oil it and shampoo it. Her skin is much more supple and she has acquired a tan, she may have gained some weight, but she's so bony it's impossible to tell at present…'

He caught her wrist in a grip which hurt and the look on his face made her catch her breath. She said once: 'I'm sorry, that was unpardonable of me—I wanted to pay you back…' Her eyes sparkled with tears. 'You came all this way to see her and I couldn't have been beastlier…'

He took her hand again, this time gently, and put it between his. He wasn't smiling, but the bleak look had gone, but when he saw the tears in her eyes he said harshly: 'Don't cry, you're not to cry.'

She sniffed. 'Well, I won't then, but I'm truly sorry…'

'You were upset about the child.' He frowned because she agreed with such haste.

'Yes, yes—I should have stopped to think, I was very silly.' She added humbly, 'If you've forgiven me I'll tell you about Diana.'

'I've forgiven you, but I shall have something to say to Mrs Kellard about turning that child away. Is she a formidable lady?'

'No, not to look at—rather wispy and fragile, if you know what I mean, and far too thin, just like…' she bit back what she had been going to say and finished lamely, 'like a pencil.'

If the doctor found this a peculiar description he didn't remark upon it, merely observed: 'I see. And Diana?'

'I think you'll see an improvement; she swims each morning and sunbathes and strolls in the gardens—her appetite isn't good, but that's partly because Mrs Kellard diets and persuades Diana to diet too.'

'But surely you have encouraged her to eat?' His voice was sharp and she flushed a little.

'Yes, Dr van Diederijk, I've done my best.'

'And you've been out? Driving round the country seeing Jerez—Cadiz?'

'Well, no, as a matter of fact we haven't been anywhere. This morning was the first time I've been away from the house.'

He was frowning again. 'But you have had your free time each day?'

Something no one had suggested, but she wasn't going to tell him that.

'Well, I haven't really needed it, you know, I've had very little to do.'

Only be at Diana's beck and call all day and sometimes at night too, she added silently.

The taxi swerved into the drive and rushed up to the house, to stop with a jolt before the entrance. The doctor got out, held the door open for Euphemia, paid the driver and stalked inside the house through the half open door. 'The sitting-room's on the left,' she told him. 'They usually have drinks about now,' and as Maria appeared from the back of the house, she skipped upstairs. A shower and a clean dress were essential. Besides, she found herself singularly reluctant to witness the doctor and Diana meeting. His face would light up as it so rarely did and Diana would rush into his arms. She got under the shower and turned it full on as though it would wash away her thoughts.

It wasn't quite like that at all. The doctor opened the door for himself, forestalling Maria by a few inches, and walked into the room. Mrs Kellard was lying as usual on her chaise-longue, a glass on the table beside her, Diana was lying on a day-bed near the open window, a glass beside her too. She was doing her nails and didn't look up at once. 'I hope you got everything I wanted,' she said. 'You've been long enough...'

She looked up then and as she was a clever young woman the utter consternation on her face was instantly masked by a delighted smile and widened eyes.

'Tane—how absolutely marvellous, what a heavenly surprise!'

The doctor stood in the centre of the room, looking at her. 'Yes, I thought I would surprise you, and I see that I have.' He walked smilingly towards her. 'You're feeling better, I hope, Diana?'

She got to her feet and came to meet him, lifting a cheek for his kiss, smiling up into his face. 'You must meet my aunt…'

Mrs Kellard made no attempt to get up. She offered a languid hand, declared that she was delighted to meet dear Diana's fiancé and that he was to stay as long as he wished. 'And pour yourself a drink, Tane—what a strange-sounding name!—lunch will be in ten minutes or so. Where's that nurse?' She looked around her, rather as though she expected Euphemia to materialise obligingly from thin air. 'We shall have to start without her.'

The doctor poured himself a small drink and sat down, choosing a chair opposite his hostess and not nearly as close to his fiancée as one would expect. 'You mean Euphemia?' he asked pleasantly. 'I brought her back with me. I met her walking down your drive with a small boy, quite badly injured, in her arms. I took them to the hospital in Jerez.'

Mrs Kellard looked uncomfortable, but only for a moment. 'Oh, yes—she came here with him, but he was quite filthy, I couldn't have allowed them to come indoors—you agreed with me, didn't you, Diana?' She smiled with studied charm. 'You above all people must know how delicate the dear girl is. She has to be shielded from anything unpleasant or dangerous to her health.'

The doctor didn't answer her. He was looking at Diana with an expressionless face, but his eyes were very bright. 'You didn't telephone?' he asked quietly.

Diana shrugged and made a pretty little face. 'Darling Tane, I don't speak Spanish.'

His voice was mild. 'You could have fetched one of the servants to telephone for you.'

Diana arranged the pleats of her cream silk dress with a careful hand. 'Darling, in all this heat? I thought I'd come here to convalesce, not run around doing other people's jobs!' She held out an arm. 'Come and sit over here by me and tell me all your news. Are you going to stay long?'

'No. Diana, have you been out at all?'

'Too hot… Euphemia makes me walk around the gardens and spend half an hour in the swimming pool, after that I'm exhausted.'

'And Euphemia? She has had time to herself, I hope?'

Diana gave a little laugh. 'Tane, darling, she does nothing all day—it must be heaven for her.'

'But she is with you all day, I presume? A companion's job consists largely of fetching and carrying, doing odd jobs that no one else wants to do, being on hand whenever she's wanted.'

'Oh, that—well, that's what she's being paid for isn't it?' She looked up as Euphemia, clean and fresh in a cotton dress, came into the room. 'Oh, there you are,' she observed. 'I'm just telling Tane what an easy life you have. Did you do my shopping?'

'No, I'm afraid not. I'll try again tomorrow morning if you don't need me then.'

Diana frowned. 'I shall want my hair washed.'

The doctor had got to his feet. 'It would do you good to wash your own hair,' he observed evenly 'and I think that

Euphemia deserves another morning off in exchange for the one she didn't get today.'

Diana's laugh sounded a little shrill. 'Oh, if you say so. After all, you'll be here. We must think of something exciting to do—just you and me.'

As they went into the dining room she said: 'You didn't say how long you were staying, Tane?'

'A couple of days. I really wanted to make arrangements for taking you back—and Euphemia of course,' he added smoothly. 'If she has no objection, and can spare another day, I thought we might go to my home and take a flight from there on the following day.'

Diana's eyes shone. 'Oh, lovely—it was such a short visit when we went there in the spring. I've thought about it a lot; all the modernising we can do, and new furnishings and curtains.'

Euphemia, sitting across the table from the doctor, saw his quick frown. Probably he lived in a nice mid Victorian house with attics and cellars, lots of heavy furniture and an old-fashioned bathroom. He would have inherited it from his parents and doubtless had never considered altering a single pot plant. He might drive a super car and dress with elegance, but just as long as he was warm and comfortable and had good meals served to him when he was home, he was probably content.

She enjoyed her lunch. There was a good deal more food on the table for a start, presumably following the adage that the way to a man's heart was through his stomach. Euphemia took full advantage of the savoury rice which flanked the dishes of salad and thinly sliced cold chicken, and when they were served with ice cream, topped with chocolate sauce and burnt almonds, she ate it with a childish pleasure not lost on the doctor. Even Diana's joking remarks about getting fat left her unmoved; it was a heavenly change from lettuce leaves and yoghurt.

She went with Diana to her room after the meal, a little surprised that that young woman intended to have her two hours' rest. Surely just for once she could have lounged on one of the garden chairs set out so invitingly in the cooler parts of the grounds? But it seemed she had no intention of changing her routine. She told the doctor that she would see him at four o'clock when they had tea on one of the terraces, advised him to lie down too, and after keeping Euphemia pottering around finding eye pads, eau-de-cologne and a book she had been reading, told her to go away.

Which Euphemia did, only too gladly. Feeling full after her unaccustomed meal, she got her writing things and went into the garden, where she was waylaid by Maria, who wanted to know about the little boy. She beamed and smiled as Euphemia told her, making her part in the affair only a small one, and then surprised her very much by taking her hands and kissing her on both cheeks.

'I know him well,' said Maria emotionally. 'He is the youngest of my nephews—he could have died.' Tears poured from her dark eyes. 'A car, they think, knocked him down and didn't stop, and he could have lain there crying…'

The tears flowed faster and Euphemia patted the plump shoulder and said, 'There, there, don't cry. He's going to get better and be all right.'

'Because of you and the kind doctor. I heard about Mrs Kellard—Manuel was in the back hall, he saw it all and heard, too, how she and the Miss would give no help at all, just because he was dirty and covered in blood. Why could they not have called one of us to telephone the hospital…?' She stopped crying for a moment, staring over Euphemia's shoulder, smiling uncertainly at someone behind them.

Euphemia whizzed round. The doctor was very close, he must have heard every word. She broke into a muddled speech, anxious to put a good light on things. 'Diana couldn't have understood—I mean, she wasn't near the door, so probably she didn't hear what it was all about—she gets upset if anyone is ill or—or…'

She stopped, halted by his cool stare. 'There is no need to cover up, Euphemia. I had a little chat with Diana and her aunt before you came down to lunch.' He grinned suddenly and looked years younger. 'I've been eavesdropping too.'

'Yes, well…can't we forget all about it? Diana isn't quite herself yet. She's much better, though, isn't she? She's so pretty. When she came to your party at Myrtle House she looked lovely…' She was aware that she was babbling, but she seemed unable to stop. Only when he said softly: 'You know, I really must agree with Dr Lopez,' did she break off in mid-sentence, her mouth slightly open. Dr Lopez had said that she was beautiful, but perhaps Dr van Diederijk didn't mean that. He went on easily, 'Shall we find somewhere shady, I could do with a nap.'

She led him to her favourite spot, a grass patch hidden away between vivid shrubs and dragon trees. 'I'm going to write these letters,' she told him, and sat down composedly, unaware of the pretty picture she made in her white dress with the hibiscus and poinsettia all round her.

The doctor lay down a few feet away, his head turned

so that he could watch her. He did it through almost closed lids so that she imagined him to be asleep, and indeed after the first glance, she didn't look at him again and got down to her letters. She had written two and was beginning on the third when he asked her suddenly, 'To whom do you write?'

'Oh, hallo, I thought you were asleep. Ellen and the boys, and a note to Mrs Cross telling her what groceries to get in. Ellen's curate is going to lunch and if I know Ellen she'll be so busy deciding what to give him to eat she'll forget things like cornflakes and Vim.' She added anxiously: 'You don't mind him going, do you? Should we have asked you first?'

He rolled over and stretched hugely. 'My dear girl, it's your home.'

'Yes, I know, but you're the tenant and I've no right…'

'For the whole of one month you have all the right in the world. Has it been worth while, Euphemia, giving up your holiday?'

She didn't look at him. 'Yes, oh yes—I've a whole week to look forward to and the others are so happy, I can never thank you enough. I expect you're longing to go back there.'

'Yes—it seems like my second home.'

'And so handy for the hospital.'

'Yes, that too, although I shall be working in Holland for several months later this year.'

She was unaware of the disappointment on her face. 'Oh—I thought you were on the consulting staff for ever…'

'Oh, but I am, several other hospitals too. I'm also a consultant at a number of hospitals in Holland, and as such I travel a good deal.'

Euphemia stared at a vivid butterfly perched near her head. 'Even when you're married?' she wanted to know.

He didn't answer, and she pinkened at the snub and bent over her writing pad again and missed his smile, and when she had finished her letter and took a quick peek at him, he was asleep again. She went indoors then to do some small job of sewing for Diana and although the doctor had tea with them, he had very little to say to her, in fact he had very little to say to Diana or Mrs Kellard either, answering them politely but not embarking upon a lengthy conversation. Nor did he evince any desire to be alone with Diana. He went for a swim after tea and then took himself off walking, not to reappear until they met before dinner in the drawing-room. Euphemia, in her long flowered skirt and embroidered cotton blouse, felt quite eclipsed by Diana's organza and Mrs Kellard's chiffon. The doctor, very correct in white dinner jacket, eyed her as she went in and she flushed a little; her outfit was charming and suited her, but she might just as well have been wearing a sheet when it came to competing with the other two women. But she wasn't competing, she told herself in bewilderment, so why this sudden urge to look her best?

Dinner was elaborate and, for once, satisfied her healthy appetite. The conversation was easy, amusing and clever, because Diana was good at that sort of thing. Euphemia, eating iced melon, chicken Kiev and lemon sorbet, spoke when spoken to and had the lowering feeling that she was not really necessary to the dinner party at all. True, the doctor addressed her from time to time, but that was only because he had probably been brought up to have good

manners. She slipped away after they had had coffee, with
the idea of telephoning the hospital to enquire after the
little boy. She would have to enlist Maria's help, of course,
which meant going along to the back of the house where
they had their quarters. She wasn't sure if Mrs Kellard
would approve of her going there on a personal errand, so
she went through the garden, round the side of the house
to where she could see the kitchen windows, already
lighted against the dusk.

She jumped visibly when the doctor's voice from somewhere close by spoke. 'If you were thinking of telephoning, I went down to the hospital this afternoon. The boy's
going to be all right, I had a look at him myself. I was about
to tell Maria.'

Euphemia let out the breath she had held out of fright.
'You startled me,' she told him accusingly. 'Yes, I was
going to ask Maria to help me phone—I'll leave you to talk
to her, and thank you for finding out.' She added a soft
'Good night', and went back the way she had come, just
in time to answer Diana's imperious demand for a lace
shawl, to be told, when she had fetched it, that she could
go to bed if she wanted. 'You must be tired after your little
adventure this morning,' declared Diana, 'and Aunt is
going to read for a while, Tane and I will take a stroll in
the gardens.'

Euphemia, wrestling with a strong wish to thump the
girl, although she wasn't sure why, bade her goodnight and
did the same to Mrs Kellard, who murmured from behind
her novel, and went to her room. It was still quite early and
she had no wish for bed; she went to sit by the window,
and presently saw Diana and the doctor strolling away

into the deepening dusk. Diana—even from that distance was obviously pulling out all the stops; the upturned face, the little helpless hand on his coat sleeve, the tinkling laugh… Euphemia ground splendid white teeth, ran a bath and lay in it, reading yesterday's *Telegraph*. The bath was far too hot and when she got out at last she looked like a beautiful lobster.

Diana had slept badly, she informed Euphemia the next morning; she had a headache and wished for nothing more than aspirin, pads soaked in cucumber over her eyes and the blinds drawn. She sounded cross too, and Euphemia wondered if she and the doctor had had words the evening before.

'Then you won't mind if I go into Jerez and do that shopping?' she asked.

'Do what you like,' said Diana crossly, 'and tell Tane not to come near me—I'll come down for lunch.'

Euphemia had had her breakfast early, so there was nothing to stop her leaving at once. Of the doctor there was no sign, so she gave Maria Diana's message and fetched her bag and left the house. Thanks to her taxi ride yesterday, she knew the way now. To walk down into the town before the day got warm was going to be pleasant. She started off for the wicket gate once more.

The doctor was waiting by it. 'Walking?' he enquired genially without bothering to answer her surprised good morning. 'We can take a taxi back.'

'I'm going to do some shopping,' she began, aware that the idea of spending an hour or so in his company was a pleasant one.

'I know, you didn't do it yesterday. It will be twice as

quick if I come with you.' He had opened the gate as he spoke and she went through, content to let the situation take care of itself.

The walk was pleasant and even when they reached the town there was a lot to see. Euphemia didn't much care for the small, mean streets tucked away almost out of sight, but as her companion pointed out she must try to see them through Spanish eyes and not compare them with a British town. 'And I can tell you of some pretty ghastly slums in London and Birmingham,' he pointed out.

'Oh, yes, I know, and I don't mean to be critical. Is that a chemist's shop over there? Because I've several things to get for Diana.'

The shopping went well, helped by a leisurely half hour at a pavement café, drinking coffee in the sun. 'Have you been here before?' asked Euphemia.

'Twice—one of the students I trained with has a practice here. You've not been to Cadiz yet, have you?'

She shook her head. 'No. I'll try before we go back, but Diana doesn't want to do any sightseeing, and I'm sure that the quiet life she's leading now does her far more good.'

His 'probably' was dry. 'Have you much more shopping?'

She looked at her list. 'No, only to go to this hair-dresser and ask for someone to go to Mrs Kellard's house and do her hair tomorrow.'

'Why can't she get to the hairdresser's?' His voice was casual.

'I don't think she's very strong,' said Euphemia politely.

The doctor looked at her. 'My dear girl, I hope you thank God on your bended knees every day of your life for being a nice healthy girl, all the right shape and size and able to do things for yourself.'

She chuckled. 'Oh, I do.' She glanced at her watch. 'Should we find the hairdresser now? I think I should be getting back…'

But it seemed that the doctor had different ideas. True, he went to the shop with her and made the necessary appointment for someone to go and see to Mrs Kellard's platinum head, but once they were on the pavement once more, he took her arm and led her away from the main street, along several narrow lanes lined with whitewashed houses until they reached a long white building with heavy gates half way down its length.

'A bodega,' he explained. 'You can't go back to England without seeing round at least one.'

He opened a little door in the gate and ushered her through into a different world. There was a lodge on one side of them, and a large low building on the other side and ahead a meticulously kept path between grass, strange coarse grass, but still grass, and everywhere there were trees and shrubs and flowers. The sun was hot now and Euphemia had forgotten to buy another hat, so that she was glad to go into the lodge with the doctor who, after a few minutes' chat with the man inside, took her outside again. 'This was founded by an Englishman, although the Spanish have taken it over now. I know the manager; we can take a look round—there are some rather splendid horses…'

'Whatever have horses got to do with it?'

'In September there is a wine festival, all the bodegas join in a procession and the wagons and carts and carriages are drawn by these horses. Let's go there first.'

They were lovely animals, with glossy coats and combed manes and tails, submitting to her pats and strokes with a lordly dignity until the doctor suggested that they might go and see where the sherry was bottled.

They climbed a staircase for this and hung over the balcony at its top the better to watch the endless chain of bottles, and presently they were joined by a young man who explained it all to them and then took them down the stairs again into a hall where he invited them to sample the sherry and delighted Euphemia by presenting her with a small bottle in a sack—to take home with her, she was told. He brought two normal sized bottles for the doctor, who tucked them under his arm with the remark that her aunt might like them.

'Aunt Thea? Well, yes, I'm sure she would—I was going to get her something…'

'Then allow me to give her these and you can find something else.' His blue eyes twinkled. 'Have another glass of sherry?'

She said yes promptly, at the same time voicing the opinion that it was a little early in the day. 'But it's so very nice,' she conceded, and allowed her glass to be filled.

They made their goodbyes presently and went out into the sun-filled street again to find a taxi. 'A pity we couldn't have stayed longer,' observed the doctor. 'The enormous sheds where they keep the vats are really something.'

'Yes—but I've seen a lot, haven't I? A little bit of Spain…'

He hailed a taxi and they got in, and when they reached the gates he told the driver not to go any further. 'The walk up the drive will clear your head,' he pointed out.

'Oh, my goodness, am I muzzy?' asked Euphemia in a panic.

He laughed. 'Of course not, but it's shady here and there's no hurry.'

She wasn't so sure about that. 'Diana will be wondering where you are.' She stopped to look at him. She said in a rush, engendered by the sherry: 'Why don't you get married? You must be earning enough to support a wife, I can't think why you don't...?'

He was staring down at her, his blue eyes hooded, 'And have you given it much thought, Euphemia?'

She went on recklessly: 'Oh, yes—you've been engaged for ages, haven't you? And it isn't as if you have to save to buy the furniture or anything like that. Surely if you fall in love with someone you know if you want to marry them...' She stopped, struck by the thought that she had fallen in love with someone, and wanted to marry him very much, only she had just discovered it, a bit late in the day, too-too late.

'Did I ever tell you that you are an abominable girl, Euphemia?'

She came back to earth with a crash. 'Oh, my goodness, yes!'

She started off again at a great rate, and neither of them spoke again.

CHAPTER SIX

EUPHEMIA WOULD have liked to have dashed straight to her room once they reached the house; the doctor hadn't spoken and she could think of nothing to say. She thought miserably that a brighter girl would have passed the whole thing off as a joke, but she wasn't feeling bright; she felt as though she had gone down a very long way in a lift unexpectedly and ended up with an almighty bump. An unpleasant bump too. Only a fool would fall in love with a man who was on the point of marrying someone else, and that someone a frightful mistake.

But luck wasn't with her. Diana called to her and she had to go to the drawing-room with her purchases and give chapter and verse for every one of them. The doctor went with her, but she avoided his eye and escaped as soon as she could, to sit in her room and wish herself anywhere but where she was. He wasn't going until the next day, somehow she must keep out of his way until then. Supposing he guessed... She rushed over to the mirror and studied her face. It looked precisely the same as usual and she sighed with relief. If she could keep it like that no one would guess that she was in love; they had no reason to suspect it even, and certainly not he. She did her face with care, tidied her hair and changed into another dress, then went back to the drawing-room. Diana and Mrs Kellard didn't look up as she went in, but the doctor did. He got up and crossed over to the drinks table, glancing at his hostess as he went. She nodded graciously and murmured: 'Oh, by all means, Tane—you're seeing to the drinks.'

He looked at Euphemia with a faint smile. 'You look as though you need something strong,' he observed blandly. 'Perhaps you overreached yourself his morning. A glass of Dry Sack, perhaps?'

'Thank you.' She was glad that her voice sounded coolly pleasant and nothing more. 'It was certainly very warm.'

Diana looked up from the embroidery she was doing. 'Well, I hope it hasn't made you tired. I was far too exhausted to wash my hair, you'll have to do it for me after lunch.' Her voice changed to a softly cajoling note. 'Tane darling, I'd love to go out to dinner this evening. Is there anywhere decent in Jerez?'

He went and sat down near her and fell to discussing where they should go, while Euphemia sat down near the window and picked up a magazine, the picture of cool calm detachment.

Diana kept her busy for an hour after lunch and when she was free she went along to her room and lay down on the bed. The room, although cool enough, seemed stuffy after the garden, but she was afraid of meeting the doctor. She thought about him instead, remembering every line and angle of his face, the way he talked and walked, and thought wonderingly that she had once disliked him, treated him in a lighthearted fashion as a tiresome person she had nothing in common with—only Myrtle House. They had that in common, and as long as he was her tenant they were bound to meet on occasion, and that wasn't to be borne if Diana was living there too as his wife.

She got up and went to hang over the little balcony, remembering that she had half planned to rescue him from Diana. She still wanted to do that but she didn't see how she could now because even to herself she would have to admit that she might stand to gain by it, and even though all was supposed to be fair in love and war she wasn't all that mean. Besides he must want to marry Diana, probably because she was such a cold fish. He might be a man who disliked demonstrative women who might interfere with his busy life, in which case Diana was just right for him.

Euphemia told herself firmly to stop thinking about the doctor. He would be gone in a few hours now and in another week she would be on the way home. She had quite forgotten what he had said about going to his own home first.

Bereft of Diana and Tane's company, Mrs Kellard decided to have dinner on a tray in her room, which left Euphemia sitting at the big table by herself. She had spent an hour or more helping Diana to achieve perfection for her evening out and then prudently slipped back to her room until she heard the Cadillac purring away from the door, and now she was enjoying her dinner. The servants, without Mrs Kellard to see what they were doing, were doing her proud; soup, cold watercress soup and delicious, *calamares fritos,* a great dish of mixed vegetables, potatoes cooked in their skins and *mojo picon* to make them piquant, followed by little tarts filled with *miel de Palma*. All very fattening and it looked gorgeous even if the main dish was squid, something she wouldn't have dreamed of eating at home. And Maria had put a bottle of dry white wine on the table and kept her glass filled. Euphemia drank three glasses and got up from the table feeling pleasantly muzzy. A little fresh air, she decided, and went outside into the warm evening to lie back on a garden chair and fell instantly asleep.

It was almost dark when she woke and there was a faint smell of a cigar tickling her nose. She jumped to her feet so quickly that she nearly fell over, and the cigar became overwhelming as the doctor took a step forward and caught her.

'My goodness!' exclaimed Euphemia in a panic. 'Whatever is the time? I fell asleep. What will Diana…I should have…'

He had made no attempt to take his arm away. 'It's almost eleven o'clock. Diana thought you had gone to bed and decided that she could manage for herself for once.' He bent his head and wrinkled his handsome nose. 'My dear girl, you've been drinking?'

'I haven't!' She was indignant. 'At least, Maria gave me some wine with my dinner—I had three glasses. It was a lovely meal, squid and that tangy sauce with the potatoes, and honey tarts for pudding.'

'It sounds better than our meal. Why did you dine alone?'

'Mrs Kellard had hers in bed.' She realised suddenly that he still had an arm round her and it must be because it was almost dark that she felt so relaxed. She added: 'I didn't mind a bit.'

He gave a little laugh. 'I don't imagine you would.' He

turned her round to face him and stood staring down at her. 'Dear little Phemie,' he said softly, and kissed her surprised mouth.

She pulled away from him and he let her go at once. 'Oh, no!' she whispered, and rushed soundlessly into the house. She had almost reached her room when Diana's door opened.

'I thought you were in bed hours ago!' Diana sounded angry.

'It was too warm.' Euphemia added a quick goodnight and closed her own door. She sat down on the bed and discovered that she was trembling, not because Diana had seen her and was probably even now having suspicious thoughts, but because Tane had kissed her. She had been kissed before on many occasions, but it had never been like that, but then he was what she supposed one would call a man of the world and was a bit of an expert. She got up and undressed and lay a long while in the bath, her head full of nonsensical thoughts which seemed to have taken over from common sense. Reality didn't seem real any more; perhaps it would be in the morning.

She woke early and indeed, in the early morning light, last night's happenings became impossible daydreams, as they really were. Euphemia went down to her breakfast and found the doctor sitting at the small table Maria always laid for her on the loggia and all the daydreams came rushing back again. Nonetheless, she wished him good morning with cool friendliness, passed the time of day with Maria and offered to pour his coffee.

'You don't mind me joining you, do you?' he wanted to know. 'Diana doesn't feel like coming down to breakfast and we'd look rather silly sitting at separate tables.'

'Of course I don't mind.' She was proud of her casual manner. Just right, she considered; friendly but cool. Rather pleased with herself, she embarked upon a one-sided conversation about the weather. There wasn't all that much to say about it, because the days were all exactly alike, unlike the weather at home, but it got her through rolls and coffee and if she got up with rather more alacrity than was polite, the doctor didn't appear to notice. She went along to see how Diana was and found her already up and dressing. Her 'good morning' was sour and she declared that she had eaten something which had disagreed with her at dinner the night before. 'That's why we came back early,' she added, giving Euphemia a sly look. 'We're going to Cadiz this morning—you'll come too, of course.'

'Me? But surely…the doctor goes this evening, doesn't he? You'll want to be on your own… I've that dress to see to—you wanted it mended as soon as possible.'

'Well, I've changed my mind—you're coming with us. Tane can drive the Cadillac and we can lunch out.'

Euphemia opened her mouth to protest again and then decided not to. If Diana was in a bad temper, it would spoil the trip for Tane. She had no idea why she was suddenly in such demand, but doubtless she would find out quickly enough.

Which she did. Sitting in the back, she was treated to a display of charm and allure the like of which she hadn't seen before. Diana, her face wreathed in smiles, cuddled up to the doctor, whispered to him, draped a skinny arm around as much of his shoulder as she could reach, and generally made an exhibition of herself. Euphemia, looking out of the window without really seeing anything, knew what it was all about. Diana must have known about last night, not all of it perhaps, but she must have guessed that Tane had met her on the patio and now she was making it very clear to Euphemia that he was hers and no mistake about it.

She wondered what the doctor thought about it, but there was no way of knowing. He drove steadily on, answering Diana's whispers in a normal voice and mostly in monosyllables. It was a pity she couldn't see his face. It had shown nothing when Diana, dragging Euphemia with her, had joined him on the patio and declared that the three of them would go. She couldn't know of his thoughts as he saw her beside Diana, her face devoid of make-up, her hair tied back, her sleeveless cotton dress showing off her brown arms and legs, but she had been very aware of her own, that she had been falling in love with him ever since they had first met, and hadn't known it. But now she did know, and she had no idea what to do about it, although how she could have been so foolish as to fall in love with such a cold, reserved man, she had no idea.

And when Diana had suddenly left them to get another sun-hat Euphemia had said hurriedly: 'I'm sorry, I didn't want to come, but Diana insisted. I only hope it won't be too hot for her…'

He had made an impatient sound. 'Diana is recovered, although she is still far too thin.'

'Well, I've done my best,' Euphemia had said reasonably, 'but it's natural that she should want to stay slim.'

'Why?' he had barked at her.

'Well, she always has been…'

'Not slim—skinny.' He had allowed his gaze to dwell on her own curvy person and she had gone red and snapped:

'Well, don't look at me, I'm plump.'

'Indeed? My eyes must be playing me false.'

Diana had joined them then, and a good thing too.

Euphemia tried to concentrate on the countryside now, although it was difficult enough with Diana carrying on the way she was. She had wanted to see Cadiz and the country around the city and she had her chance. Vine-covered plains stretched to the horizon, dotted with small white-washed houses and almost no trees, and these small umbrella shapes—a little disappointing. And the other side, with the sea in the distance, was disappointing too— salt flats and narrow waterways and here and there a small copse of the same small trees. Euphemia could see the out-skirts of Cadiz ahead now, all the paraphernalia of docks; cranes and ships and large sheds which housed she knew not what. They could have been anywhere in the world.

The doctor spoke to her over his shoulder. 'Disappointed, Euphemia? This is the wrong end—the docks and port. We're going into the city in a few moments now.'

He drove through an ancient gateway piercing the great walls of the old city and slowed the car, so that she had time to peer down the narrow crowded streets on either side of them. She would have liked to have got out and walked, but he swept on, through another gate and into a boulevard with the sea on one side, bordered by beautifully kept gardens and, on the other, great mansions, cheek by jowl with blocks of modern flats. Everything was clean and splendid and colourful, contrasting strongly with the narrow streets they had just left. Euphemia would have liked to have talked about it, but Diana was saying that she simply had to have coffee and did Tane know of a decent café?

He parked presently before a large modern restaurant and they had their coffee sitting on the pavement outside, but there was no chance to ask questions then, either, because Diana kept up a careless flow of talk which gave no one else a chance to say anything. It was clever talk, amusing and witty and delivered in an artless manner which Euphemia had to admire. Whether the doctor admired it or not was difficult to tell. He sat almost silent, looking bland and smiling faintly from time to time.

Diana finished her coffee first. 'Well, if this is Cadiz, I don't think I want to see any more of it, unless there are some decent shops.'

'Several—there are some splendid churches and several magnificent buildings. It's one of the oldest cities in Europe and built by the Phoenicians about 1100 BC. It's a fortress town…'

Diana hunched a shoulder. 'Oh, for heaven's sake, Tane, who wants to know all that old rubbish!' She put a hand on his arm and smiled up at him. 'Couldn't we just take a quick peep at the shops—you haven't bought me a present for ages.'

He was sitting back with his eyes half closed. 'And what do you wish me to buy you, Diana?'

She pouted prettily. 'I haven't a decent rag to my back, a new dress would be fun.' And when he got up with a cheerful, 'Let's go, then,' she shot Euphemia a look of triumph.

'There's a boutique Aunt was telling me about, it's near some church or other.'

The doctor knew where it was. He parked the car outside the elegant little shop, leaned across Diana to open her door and then got out himself, but when he went to open the door for Euphemia Diana said sharply: 'Oh, Euphemia won't want to come inside—clothes don't seem to interest her, she can stay in the car.' And when the doctor didn't move, 'Tane, you must come in with me, I can't speak a word of Spanish.'

He went inside with her and Euphemia sat and looked out of the window at the busy street, full of expensive shops and cafés and mostly modern. If only they had let her go off on her own; she wasn't having much luck with her sightseeing. She sat back and closed her eyes and two tears trickled forlornly down her cheeks.

'Sorry about this,' said the doctor, and she opened her eyes again to see him, head and shoulders through the window, within inches of her. He saw the tears and she was eternally grateful to him for pretending not to. 'It's a wonderful city, but you need to potter around on foot. That's what you would have liked to do, wasn't it?'

She nodded, 'Yes,' and wiped away the tears with what she hoped was a careless gesture of a hand.

'And another thing, I don't know a great deal about such things, but it seems to me that clothes interest you very much. You dress very well.'

He was being kind and she could have flung her arms around his neck. She managed a bright smile. 'Thank you—but on a nurse's salary? Though I love clothes.' She drew a breath and went on steadily: 'I think Diana has beautiful clothes and she wears them well. You must be proud of her.'

He didn't answer, and she looked up to find him staring at her unsmilingly. 'You'll like my home, Euphemia,' he said at length, and smiled then. 'I'd better go and settle the bills, I suppose. There was no point in staying in the shop, they all spoke English.'

He turned away and presently emerged with Diana and a salesgirl carrying a dress box. All the way back Diana chattered about the dress she had bought, describing it in detail, pretending to be shocked at its price. 'Don't you wish you had someone to buy you some decent clothes?' she asked Euphemia.

Her rudeness didn't deserve an answer and Euphemia didn't give one.

They lunched at the villa after all, with Diana dominating the talk at table and then declaring that she wouldn't rest after lunch as Tane would have to leave directly after tea. She carried him off to the garden, and when Euphemia went down to the drawing-room for tea it was to find Mrs Kellard lying back as usual and to be told that Diana and Tane were having theirs in the garden, so she drank her own tea quickly and went back to her room, suddenly anxious not to see the doctor again.

Her room overlooked the garden at the side of the house. She heard the Cadillac at the front door, heard the doctor's voice and Diana's answering him and a car door bang, but she was too far away to hear what was said. She went back to her chair and got on with the sewing of Diana's torn dress.

There was a week left. She threw herself whole-heartedly into the fulfilling of her share of the bargain. She brushed Diana's hair until it gleamed, rubbed in creams and lotions, persuaded her to swim and to eat more, perversely anxious that she should look her very best for the doctor when he returned. And she was largely successful. Diana was still like a beanpole, but at least she had a healthy colour and a faint tan. She had chosen to wear a silk trouser suit in which to greet him when he arrived and Euphemia, watching from the sitting-room window, had to admit that she looked remarkably pretty. But she didn't wait to see the doctor greet her as he got out of the car. She had had a week in which to pull herself together and she had done it very well.

In due course, just before dinner, she went down to the drawing-room and greeted him quietly. He looked tired, she thought. If they had been on their own she would have asked him about his work, but Diana was in full spate, rattling on about this and that and the other thing, not waiting for his replies, intent upon attracting attention to herself. Euphemia wondered if she knew that the doctor wasn't really listening to her.

They left the next morning and Euphemia, given two fingers of Mrs Kellard's hand in a tepid farewell, was grateful for Maria's warm kiss. She got into the back of the Cadillac with a sulky Diana and didn't look back, because she didn't mind if she never saw the villa again. Instead she studied the doctor's head, even from the back it was worth looking at.

But it was a pointless exercise. She began to think about the week ahead of her at Myrtle House. It would be fun to be home again with Ellen and the boys; she had had letters from them, spilling over with news about the house and the garden and Mrs Cross, just as though they still lived there. Euphemia began to ponder the future. The doctor had an agreement for a year and almost two months of that had gone already. It wasn't likely that Diana would want to live there permanently, so that she would have to find someone else, someone who would want it for a longer period, or perhaps she should sell it and buy a smaller house somewhere close by, where they could all live. There might be money over too…

She hardly noticed going through Customs and boarding the plane; her head was still full of ways and means. They were airborne, she sitting behind the other two, when the doctor turned round to ask if she was quite comfortable. 'And what's on your mind, Euphemia?' he asked softly. 'You're not with us, are you?'

She assured him that she was very comfortable adding that she was busy thinking.

'What about, I wonder?'

She met his intent blue eyes briefly. 'Nothing important,' she assured him.

What with coffee and sandwiches, magazines and newspapers, a garrulous old lady sitting next to her and Diana feeling sick, the flight went quickly, and they were taxiing towards Schiphol airport before she had settled down to do anything, much less have a good think. Euphemia followed Diana off the plane and the doctor shepherded them both through the Customs, saw that their luggage was collected and led them to the entrance.

The Bentley was parked within a few feet with a stolid youngish man sitting at the wheel. He got out when he saw them, greeted the doctor with a broad grin, ducked his head to Diana, who ignored him, and did the same to Euphemia, who smiled back and said, 'Hullo'. The man dealt with the luggage, ushered them into the back of the car and then got in beside the driver's seat where the doctor was already.

Had they far to go? Euphemia asked Diana.

'Somewhere near Hilversum, I don't know how far.'

'About half an hour,' said the doctor over his shoulder as he joined the motorway. He turned off on a roundabout presently and joined another motorway going south, then left that too to take a quieter road which presently gave them a glimpse of water. 'Loenerveensche Plas', he informed them. 'I daresay you remember it, Diana.'

'Well, I don't—I saw so many lakes last time. Are we nearly there? I've a most frightful headache.'

Euphemia, well prepared, handed eau-de-cologne sachets and promised aspirin as soon as they arrived, then took a look at the lake. There were a number of sailing boats on it and it looked peaceful and pleasant in the sunshine. The country had altered too, the flat green fields had given way to heath and woodland, and when the doctor took a narrow road running away from the water the woods thickened so that they came to the very edge and instead of the neat farmhouses with their huge barns there were elegant villas not wholly visible through the trees.

The road was a brick one and narrow and there was almost no traffic, and although she had noticed a signpost to Hilversum, Euphemia doubted if it went to that town. More probably it would end at a main road. They went round a wide curve and she saw a village at the end of it— a small village, more of a hamlet, although it had a high-steepled church at its centre. The doctor had slowed to go past its few cottages, but once on the other side of the green he gave the car its head once more, hardly slackening speed as he turned it into a drive, past a gatehouse guarding open wrought iron gates. Euphemia was still staring at them from the back window when Diana said: 'I shall see that those gates are kept shut when we're living here,' to which remark the doctor made no answer. Perhaps he hadn't heard.

The drive ran straight as a ruler to the house—a large square edifice of the William and Mary period, its red brick glowing in the sun, its tall wide windows sparkling, the flowers in the beds arranged symmetrically around it, adding a rainbow of colour. Euphemia sighed soundlessly. She had guessed that the doctor was comfortably off and that he probably lived in a villa of some sort, but she hadn't expected this. He must be rich, taking it all for granted. No wonder he was going to marry Diana! She would be so right for such a splendid place; it wouldn't be just a question of falling in love with some girl, she would have to be able to cope with his way of living too. Euphemia had no doubt that Diana would fill the bill admirably.

The doctor brought the Bentley to a purring halt before the shallow steps and the double doors at their top were opened as he did so. The man who did it had one arm, Euphemia noted with interest as she got out and followed the others up the steps, going slowly so that she could have a good look round as she went. She found the doctor waiting patiently in the doorway. 'This is Domus,' he told her, and she shook hands, careful to do it left-handed to accommodate Domus's one arm, and wishing that she might be left alone for just a few minutes to gaze round the hall, a circular apartment with a broad staircase facing the door and a gallery above. But she was given no chance. She and Diana were swept towards a pair of doors, embellished with marquetry and massive brass handles, and urged to go through them.

The room was large and lofty and splendidly furnished, and yet it gave the instant impression of being lived in. There were books and magazines and things scattered around, a dog of no known breed prancing to meet them and a cat sitting cosily in the middle of one of the elegant sofas. Euphemia smiled, feeling instantly at home, and became aware that there were two people in the room— an elderly man sitting in a winged chair by one of the open windows and a plump little lady, middle-aged, but still pretty with grey hair and blue eyes, who jumped to her feet and cried: 'Tane, how lovely to see you—and Diana, of course.' Her eyes slid to Euphemia and her face broke into a wide smile. 'And this is Euphemia.'

Her son gave her a bearlike hug. 'You didn't mind coming over, Mama?'

'It seemed a good opportunity.'

He smiled at her as if he were sharing a secret with her and turned to shake his father's hand, before drawing Diana forward. 'You know Diana, of course, and this is Euphemia—my mother and father. They live a few miles away and since I shan't be home for a few weeks they've come over for dinner this evening.'

Euphemia liked them both, but beyond greeting them pleasantly and uttering a few conventional remarks, she stayed quiet. After all, it was Diana's right to take the stage. Which she had done, instantly and with an expertise which Euphemia couldn't help but admire. She chattered on and on, being amusing and wistful by turns, hardly pausing for anyone else to say anything, making the mumps sound like a dreaded plague she had barely escaped from with her life. She gave an account of her stay at Jerez which, although amusing, bore little semblance to the truth, and ignored Euphemia completely. It was when the tea tray was brought in that she paused, long enough for Mevrouw van Diederijk to take the conversation into her own hands, and this time Euphemia was included. Not that they talked about anything much; it was the gentle kind of conversation her own friends indulged in over a cup of tea, neither witty nor clever, and she was perfectly at home in it, whereas Diana, no longer the centre of interest, sat sullenly, saying almost nothing. The elegant little meal was hardly over when she put down her cup.

'You'll have to excuse me, I've got a headache and I must lie down. If I could go up to my room? Euphemia, come with me and find the aspirin, and you can unpack my overnight bag at the same time.'

There was a small silence as Euphemia got to her feet. 'Yes, of course,' she said easily. 'It's been quite a journey, hasn't it?' She looked at Mevrouw van Diederijk. 'You won't mind, *mevrouw?*' She smiled nicely at her, thinking what a dear she was. 'You'll be glad to have a talk with your son.'

Mevrouw van Diederijk's eyes twinkled. 'As a matter of fact I shall, my dear, but I hope you will come down as soon as you can and join us.'

Her husband had got to his feet. 'I met your father once, years ago,' he boomed at her, his English as good as his wife's, although the accent was more pronounced. 'We must have a talk.'

Euphemia murmured and hurried to the door because she could see Diana was getting impatient. As she reached it Diana said: 'Tane, why do you keep all this ghastly furniture?' She tapped him playfully on the sleeve. 'Just wait

till I get my hands on this place! I'm going to throw it all
into the attics—we'll have some decent modern pieces.'

'Over my dead body,' said the doctor quietly, and
Diana laughed. Euphemia, glancing into his face, saw
that he meant it.

They went first to Diana's room, led there by a cheerful
round body who nodded and smiled to make up for her
lack of English and showed them into a room at the side
of the house. It was large, with windows overlooking the
garden, and furnished rather heavily with a mahogany bed
and bow-fronted chest, as well as an enormous dressing
table and a couple of small velvet-covered chairs. Diana
flung herself down on the bed and told Euphemia to draw
the curtains. 'Why on earth did Tane have to invite his
parents here today?' she demanded. 'They're so dull and
straitlaced they bore me. I'll take care that they don't come
too often once we're married.' She swallowed the aspirins
Euphemia was holding out. 'Not that I intend to live here
for more than a week or two each year, buried in the
country. I shall tell Tane so too. We can live in London just
as well—after all, he works there almost as much as he
does here.'

To all of which Euphemia said nothing. She very much
doubted if Tane would like any of the changes with which
Diana was going to alter his life, but it was hardly her
business to say so, and if he wanted this girl for his wife
that wasn't her business either. She said woodenly: 'I'll
unpack later, you'll be able to sleep a little now, I expect,'
and got herself out of the room.

The little round woman was waiting for her and led her
back along the gallery to the other side of the house, and

opened the door of a room at the front of the house this time—a much smaller room, but so pretty that Euphemia exclaimed over it. It had two tall windows leading on to a small balcony and the furniture was white with pink and blue brocade curtains and bedspread, pink lampshades and a thickly piled carpet on the floor. The bathroom was pink too, and equipped with everything she could have asked for. She smiled her thanks at the little woman who crossed the room and opened a wall closet and waved a hand inside. Euphemia's few things had been unpacked and hung away. She prowled round the delightful room when she was left on her own and decided that it must have belonged to a daughter of the family. It was a girl's room, a family room too, lovingly cared for. She sniffed at the roses on the table by the bed, combed her hair and did her face, then went downstairs.

The doctor was lounging in the hall. 'My mother and father are having a rest before dinner and it's too early to change, so I thought you might like to see something of the house.'

She had been unable to stop the smile which curved her mouth at the sight of him, but she managed to keep her voice coolly friendly.

'I should like that very much.' She was standing beside him now at the foot of the stairs. 'It's very beautiful—if it were mine I wouldn't want to leave it.'

He said, apologetically almost: 'I do have my work,' and bent to pull the dog's ears. 'I suppose I could rearrange that so that I could live here permanently.'

Euphemia began: 'But Di...' and stopped, not quite in time, for he took her up. 'Diana doesn't like it here.' His voice was silky, offering a challenge, she thought, so she said hastily: 'I like your dog—what's his name?'

'Boris. Where would you like to start?'

'I've no idea.'

'Then the little sitting-room, I think. Have you all you want in your room?' He sounded a polite host, and she answered just as politely.

'Yes, thank you. It's such a pretty room, too. And it looks lived in, if you know what I mean.'

'It's my youngest sister's room, I thought you might like it.' He opened a door on the opposite side of the hall. 'In here.'

It was a small room as rooms went in that large house, with a little bay window with a cushioned window seat, a small chimneypiece and several comfortable chairs and tables, a lovely glass-fronted cabinet along one wall and a small upright piano against the other. 'Oh, I like it!' declared Euphemia. 'It's cosy.'

'And old-fashioned?' It was a question.

'Not in the least—one could sit here and sew or play the piano or play cards with the children.' She stopped, because her imagination was running away with her.

'Go on,' prompted the doctor softly.

She moved away and bent to look at the silver on display in the cabinet, not looking at him. 'No,' she said, 'I was only remembering when we were all children.'

'You were happy? So was I.' His voice was suddenly harsh. 'I hope my children will be as happy.'

She stared up at him, wondering if Diana had told him that she didn't intend to have any, not even one. Her kind heart was wrung with pity for him. Now that she'd got to know him, he wasn't cold and arrogant and tiresome at all, he was like any other man wanting a wife and children. Probably, once one had got behind that reserve of his, he was quite fun… She wished she didn't love him quite so much, but just being with him for an hour was wonderful, and she must be thankful for small mercies.

She still didn't think that he loved Diana, not enough to marry the girl, but it seemed equally obvious that he was going to marry her anyway, and she could quite see why. She stood looking at a very beautiful silver loving cup, her back to him, so far away in her thoughts that she uttered them aloud: 'Everything's such a muddle!'

CHAPTER SEVEN

'AND WHAT EXACTLY do you mean by that?'

The doctor had whisked her round and held her in front of him, his hands still on her shoulders.

Euphemia said wildly: 'Nothing, oh, nothing...I was thinking out loud—it slipped out. The ward—I was worrying about the ward...'

He looked so ferocious that she pulled away from him, but was unable to budge an inch. 'Don't lie to me of all people, Phemie.'

He was right, of course, although he couldn't know why she found it almost impossible to lie to him. 'I'm sorry,' she told him. 'It was a lie. It's not the ward, it's something private I can't talk about.'

He dropped a light kiss on the top of her head. 'That's better. Promise me you'll not do that again.' His blue eyes searched her face. 'I'll never lie to you, Euphemia, because I wouldn't be able to.' His hands dropped from her shoulders and he smiled. 'I'm glad you like this room, I use it a great deal when I'm home. The house is rather large just for one...'

She said eagerly: 'Oh, of course it is, it needs some

children,' and then stopped again and went on awkwardly: 'Are you home very much?'

'Not as much as I used to be. Now that I live at Myrtle House I'm perfectly content to spend my weekends and free days there.'

They were crossing the hall again towards another big double doorway.

'Oh yes, because of Diana. I do hope she'll be happy there.' She glanced at him as she spoke, hopeful of an answer, but all she got was, 'Don't fish, Euphemia,' as he opened the doors and they went into the dining-room.

This was large and on the gloomy side, its heavy mahogany table ringed with a dozen chairs, its massive sideboard laden with chafing dishes, muffin dishes, dishes with silver covers, an enormous tray laden with a silver coffee service.

'Heavens!' cried Euphemia, quite overcome with so much grandeur, and the doctor laughed.

'Overwhelming, isn't it? But I haven't the heart to banish them to the store rooms—besides, Domus loves cleaning them.'

'Why has he only got one arm?'

'He lost the other during the war. I got him fitted with an artificial arm, but he only wears it on Sunday when he goes to church.'

He crossed the room and went to stand before a wall covered in portraits. 'Come over here and look at some of these paintings—all family.'

'The nose gets handed down, doesn't it?' observed Euphemia. She paused in front of a small portrait of a young woman dressed in the style of the thirties. 'That is

your mother, isn't it? She's pretty.' She turned round to
look at him. 'Perhaps I shouldn't have said that, but I mean
it, I wasn't just trying to—curry favour.'

'I know that. She was very pretty when she was
younger, and I think she still is. My father is of the same
opinion.'

'He's nice too. Who is this man with the funny hat and
the little dog?'

'Another Tane, a dandy in his day, I believe, which may
account for the hat.'

Euphemia laughed. 'It's a dear little dog, though I'd
rather have Boris.'

The beast, hearing his name, wreathed himself round
her, his tongue hanging out, and she bent to pat him. Just
for the moment she was quite happy; somehow when she
was with Tane she didn't bother about the future.

They wandered all over the house, strolling in and out
of rooms, some used, some not, though it was hard to tell
the difference because they were all maintained to perfection. They had done the ground floor thoroughly and were
on their way upstairs when the *Stoelklok* on the wall below
them struck the hour.

'Seven o'clock? It can't be—oh, my goodness,
whatever time do you have dinner?—and I promised I'd
wake Diana!' Euphemia went bounding up the remainder
of the staircase and was caught at the top by the doctor's
long arm from behind her.

'Dinner is at eight, and don't put on anything too grand.
Mother's not changing.'

'No, all right. Thank you for showing me your house—
it's so beautiful.' She said suddenly, urgently, and not aware

that she called him by name, 'Tane, you must marry soon, it's all being wasted.'

He didn't smile, only his eyes gleamed with amusement. 'Funny you should say that, I shall marry at the first opportunity; I decided that quite recently.' He put out a finger and touched her cheek gently. 'Come down for drinks as soon as you are ready.'

Diana was still dozing, but she woke in a temper, declaring that she was still tired. 'And not nearly enough time to change for the evening,' she grumbled, and when Euphemia pointed out that there was no need to do more than change into a short dress, she lifted a shoulder and said she would wear exactly what she wanted. Euphemia went away then to her own room and showered and put on a plain pale cotton dress which, while not this year's, was still something to be reckoned with, and went back to Diana's room, to find her preening herself before the pier glass. She was wearing an orange brocade jump-suit and a great many gold bangles.

'Pretty stunning, isn't it?' she wanted to know.

'It's spectacular,' agreed Euphemia, and added carefully: 'It's a bit dressed up for this evening, isn't it? Tane said his mother wouldn't be changing…'

Diana turned round to look at her. 'Who said you could call him Tane?' She gave a sniggering laugh. 'Don't tell me that the starchy Miss Blackstock has been turned on at last, and what a pity he doesn't even know you're there…' She turned back to the mirror. 'And I'll wear what I damn well please. I'm not ready—go on down do.'

So Euphemia went downstairs to the drawing-room, where the doctor and his parents had been joined by a guest; a rather stout man of middle height, with a florid face and prominent blue eyes. He was introduced as Cor de Vries, and the doctor said easily, 'Cor met Diana when she was here some months ago and it seems a good opportunity to renew their acquaintance.'

Euphemia murmured politely and thought Cor to be pompous, wondering what there was about him that could make him a friend of Tane. Chalk and cheese, she thought, and went and sat between the doctor's parents.

They were telling her of their own home, only a few miles away, when the door opened and Diana came in. Old Mijnheer van Diederijk paused for a second at the sight of her, then went on with what he was saying, and his wife's face didn't alter, although Euphemia had heard the quick breath. As for the doctor, he went forward to meet Diana without a comment, saying cheerfully that he knew that she would be delighted to meet Cor again. 'You got on very well,' he commented. 'I hope you'll become fast friends.'

He got Diana a drink, stayed talking to the two of them for a few minutes and then joined his parents and Euphemia.

They went into dinner presently and Euphemia, taking a close look at Cor de Vries, decided that he wasn't quite her cup of tea, although Diana appeared to find him a delightful companion. He tended to monopolise the conversation, making pompous jokes and laughing heartily at them, and talking about himself, so that presently she decided that he was a conceited bore, an opinion certainly not shared by Diana. The girl was positively animated, laughing with him, listening to his boasting, taking only a small part in the general conversation. Euphemia, keeping up her end with the small talk, wondered how the doctor could stand the man, and surely he would object to Diana being monopolised so blatantly. If he did, he was concealing it admirably.

They returned to the drawing-room for coffee when the leisurely meal was finished, and Euphemia, remembering the sparse meals at Jerez, sighed happily at the memory of lobster soup, duckling cooked in brandy and Curaçao and served with fresh pineapple, the *artichaut Clamart,* the *pommes de terre Beray,* and all these culinary masterpieces topped with a purée of chestnuts with whipped cream. She found the doctor beside her as they crossed the hall and smiled widely at him. 'What a heavenly meal,' she told him, 'after all those cold chickens and lettuce leaves, and I'm not sure what I was drinking, but it was quite delicious.'

He dropped an arm lightly round her shoulders and her heart doubled its beat and colour crept treacherously into her face. 'Glad you enjoyed it,' he observed. 'You must come and meet Martje, my cook—she's always complaining that she hasn't enough work to do.'

He saw her to a chair near his mother and drifted away, and presently she heard him laughing with Diana and Cor de Vries at the other end of the room. It was late when Cor declared that he must leave. He bade everyone a pompous goodbye and Tane and Diana went with him to the door and didn't come back. Euphemia could hear Diana's trilling laugh from somewhere outside and after a little while the doctor came indoors again to join them. 'Diana's gone to bed,' he told them. 'Euphemia, I suggest that you do the same, you must be tired.'

She got quickly to her feet, blushing a little because of course he wanted her out of the way so that he could talk to his parents. She said her goodnights composedly, politely and genuinely regretful that she wouldn't see the doctor's parents again, and made for the door. The doctor reached it at the same time and went into the hall with her.

'What did you think of de Vries?' he asked her.

She hadn't expected that and she hesitated, trying to find the right answer. 'He seemed very nice,' she said lamely.

The doctor gave a crack of laughter. 'My dear girl, is that all you can say about him? Or are you afraid of offending me?' He glanced down at her. 'Yes, that's it, isn't it?'

'Well—yes, I thought he was a friend of yours and that you liked him.'

'Phemie, my dear, he is an unutterable bore and so full of himself it's a wonder he doesn't burst. I cannot stand him at any price.'

'Oh—then why…?' She stopped; she was being nosey and would get a snub for it.

'I'm not going to tell you that.' He bent and kissed her gently. 'Goodnight, Euphemia.'

His face was very close. She mumbled: 'You mustn't— oh, you mustn't,' and kissed him back.

She should have slept dreamlessly in her lovely room; instead she tossed and turned, her head crammed to bursting with incoherent thoughts, none of which made sense. Thank heaven, she muttered over and over again, that tomorrow would see the last of him. Once at Heathrow she could say her goodbyes and that would be that. She had quite forgotten that she would see him often enough at the hospital. As it was, comforted by the thought that she would forget him as from the very next day, she dropped off into an uneasy doze, only to wake to the realisation that life without him would be unthinkable.

It was still very early, but she knew she wouldn't sleep again. She got out of bed and looked out of the window at the garden below, beautiful in the pearly morning light. You fool, she told herself savagely, where's your pride? What would Father have said? Her father, having been a soldier, would have said, 'All's fair in love and war!' which didn't seem the right answer.

Euphemia leaned out as far as she could to view the great expanse of garden round the house, grateful for the cool morning breeze. 'And to think that I actually considered finding a way to stop him marrying Diana!' she muttered. 'I must have been mad—and conceited.'

She withdrew her person from the rather hazardous angle at which she had been leaning, then poked her head out again as the doctor called her name.

He was below her window, in slacks and a thin sweater, Boris weaving in and around his legs. 'Come on down, it's heavenly, and I want to show you the garden.'

'No,' said Euphemia, and withdrew her head, only to put it out again because Boris barked. He had a loud bark and was proud of it, and since his master did nothing to stop him, he went on making a terrible noise.

'Be quiet, do!' hissed Euphemia. 'You'll wake everyone up.'

'Then you'd better come down, because he won't stop once he's started,' observed the doctor cheerfully.

'You should train him.' She had to raise her voice to be heard above the din. 'All right, but I'll be ten minutes.' She added carefully: 'Wouldn't Diana like to…'

'Don't be silly,' he admonished her. 'She never lifts her head off the pillow before ten o'clock.'

Euphemia showered, threw on her clothes, tied her hair back and thrust her feet into sandals, telling herself all the time that she was behaving badly; that Diana certainly wouldn't like it if she knew, and that she wasn't being fair to the girl. Not that she had any chance of diverting Tane's attention. All the same, although it wasn't war, it was certainly love, so fairness didn't come into it. She crept through the wide corridors and down the stairs and out into the garden through the garden doors, where she found Tane and Boris waiting.

She said with dignity: 'Good morning. I only came because Boris was making such a din.' She glanced at him as she said it and saw the smile on his face; it wasn't a nasty smile at all, it was a smile to set a girl's heart thumping. She prudently looked away and remarked that it was a beautiful morning.

'Better than at the Villa,' he agreed. 'Come and see the roses. When I was at Myrtle House the garden there was a riot of colour.'

'Yes, it looks lovely in the summer—I asked the boys to keep it in good order for you. You'll be going back there in eight days' time?'

He nodded. 'I have to go on to Birmingham tomorrow and then I shall be back here for a couple of days—which reminds me, your fees have been sent to Myrtle House.'

He took her arm and guided her down a narrow grass

path between high hedges; it opened on to a circular bed, crammed with roses, and Euphemia exclaimed with delight. They strolled round it, pausing to examine the specimens which caught her eye, and they had almost completed the full circle when the doctor asked: 'Had you ever thought of selling Myrtle House, Euphemia?'

She looked at him in horror. 'No—at least, when Father died and I discovered that we hadn't any money, I thought I'd have to do that, but now I think I can manage. When you go, I'll have to find another tenant, of course, but as long as I can let it to someone that will pay for the mortgage. It simply mustn't go out of the family.'

'And how many more years has the mortgage to run?' And when she told him: 'A good slice of your life, Euphemia—is it worth it?'

She bent to sniff at the superb example of Wendy Cussons. 'Yes, of course it's worth it; I want the boys to have it. Ellen will marry her curate, I feel sure, and the mortgage will be paid by the time Nicky marries. If he doesn't then he and Billy can live there…'

'And you?'

'Oh, I'll be all right—I've got a good job.'

'You have an aversion to marriage?'

She frowned a little, disliking the blandness of his voice.

'Of course not, but—no one's asked me since Father died and I've no intention of burdening anyone with things like a mortgage.'

'Is there someone you would like to marry?' he persisted.

Euphemia wandered on a few paces and examined a charming group of miniature roses; if she said yes he would want to know who, and he had a tiresome way of wearing one down…and if she said no that would be a lie, and she found she couldn't tell him lies easily. 'Your roses are really magnificent,' she observed in a voice reminiscent of the lady of the manor at the local flower show.

He laughed. 'Put in my place, am I? Do I know him?'

She didn't quite meet his eyes. 'I'm not going to answer that either.'

He took her arm. 'There's rather a nice pond at the end of this path. I can find out easily enough, you know.'

Her voice shook a little. 'But if I ask you not to, you won't, will you?'

They had reached the pond, ringed with water flowers and ferns and housing a number of small water fowl. The doctor took his hand from her arm and flung an arm around her shoulders. 'I can't think why you object so strongly—after all, I have an interest in you. You're my landlady—and this man, whoever he is, might decide to buy the house and then where should I be?'

She said earnestly: 'I promise you that won't happen,' and then forgetting everything else but his comfortable presence, 'He won't ever marry me. He's…he's…'

'Ah, the eternal triangle.' His voice was soothing and just sufficiently impersonal, although there was a glint of laughter in his eyes. 'But take heart, Phemie, there is nearly always a way out.'

'Not for me, there isn't. Isn't that a mandarin duck in those reeds?'

'Yes, there are a pair—nice, aren't they? In the cold weather we get any number of visitors. Some of them come back year after year, some of them stay—there are quite a variety here. Kingfishers too. This pond empties into a stream at the boundary of the grounds—there is some good fishing to be had.'

He went on to talk about the surrounding countryside and told her something of the history of the house as they walked back again, to be met at the side door by Domus, informing them that breakfast was in the small dining-room if they cared to have it.

Love, thought Euphemia, tucking in to rolls and toast and croissants spread with ham and cheese and black cherry jam, and drinking several cups of delicious coffee, was supposed to take your appetite away; hers had never been better.

It was still early. They had almost finished their breakfast when Tane's mother and father joined them. There was no sign of Diana, and when Mevrouw van Diederijk wanted to know where she was, Domus murmured in her ear, something which surprised her, for she observed: 'Well, I suppose she is tired and she told me that she had been very ill with the mumps—but she has had two weeks' complete rest.' The lady's gentle voice conveyed the suggestion that she herself had never needed two weeks' rest, and she went on in a tone of satisfaction. 'You were up early, Euphemia, I hope it wasn't because you couldn't sleep?'

'I like the early morning,' Euphemia told her, 'even when I've slept all night.' She looked up as she spoke and found the doctor's eye bent upon her, so that she instantly felt guilty of telling a fib about sleeping well and went pink.

There was time to go to the kitchens and meet the doctor's cook after breakfast, although Euphemia had hesitated; she had taken up most of his morning so far, she didn't think Diana would like it if he were absent when she got downstairs. But he had swept her along, through the hall and the green baize door at the back of that noble apartment, and she had found herself in the kind of kitchen any woman would have envied. It was very large and at a first glance looked old-fashioned, with its scrubbed table in the centre and a vast dresser against one wall, but tucked away so as not to spoil the homely effect were all the modern gadgets one could wish for. Moreover, there was a second smaller room where the washing up was done, and that in its turn led to a small pantry where the china and silver were kept. Euphemia browsed happily with the cheerful Martje in attendance, while the doctor sat on the table swinging his long legs and eating the cheese straws his cook had just fetched from the oven.

They had almost finished their coffee in the small sitting room when Diana joined them, and within minutes there was a phone call for her from Cor de Vries. Euphemia could hear her laughing and chattering away with an animation she seldom showed with Tane and stole a look at his face to see how he was reacting to that. He certainly was not annoyed or disturbed; indeed, he looked totally uninterested, and yet she had the strange feeling that he was pleased about something.

The doctor's parents left directly after an early lunch, and they themselves left for Schiphol half an hour after that. The doctor drove with Dirk the chauffeur sitting beside him and the two girls in the back of the Bentley, which Dirk would drive back to his home: 'Because I'm returning tomorrow evening and it's not worth taking the car for such a short time,' he explained.

Euphemia, twisting round to get a last view of the house, told herself that she should feel pleased about that, and instead was mortified to feel a knot of tears in her throat. In vain she thought about spending the next week at Myrtle House and all the things she was going to do with the money she had earned. The one ray of happiness she felt was that Tane wasn't going to stay at Diana's house, but that was short-lived, for presently he said over his shoulder: 'I'd like to come up and see you, Diana—some time at the end of the week, perhaps?'

Diana was admiring the diamond ring on her engagement finger. 'Why not?' she agreed. 'Only do telephone first, won't you? Now I'm so much better I shall be going out a good deal.'

He grunted a reply and Euphemia looked lovingly at the back of his head and wished he would say the same thing to her, which was so silly that she smiled, only to see his eyes fixed on her in the driving mirror, so she turned sideways and looked out of the window and didn't speak again until they arrived at Schiphol. Then it was Customs and passports and a bare five minutes to wait before their flight was called, so that they were airborne before she had had time to feel regret at leaving Holland.

She stared out of the window watching the green fields getting farther and farther away and the houses turning into dolls' houses. It was unlikely she would ever go back there and she had hardly glimpsed it, only Tane's home, and that she wouldn't forget in a hurry. She closed her eyes and pretended to sleep and didn't open them again until the stewardess brought coffee, and soon after that they were at Heathrow. Diana and the doctor had been sitting across the aisle to her and she had been aware of their voices. They had talked a lot—probably the wedding arrangements, making plans to meet again. She followed them out of the plane and through the now familiar routine of luggage and passports and Customs and found herself standing with them outside the airport. But only for a moment; they were joined by Diana's father, almost at once, an elderly worried-looking man, who kissed her gingerly, shook the doctor's hand and looked vaguely at Euphemia, saying: 'Oh, yes, of course, the nurse,' and then turned back to Tane. 'You'll come back with Diana?' he asked.

'I'm afraid I've an appointment for the early evening at the hospital and I'm going back tomorrow morning.'

Sir Arthur Sibley turned to Euphemia. 'And you, Nurse—can we drop you off?'

Diana, saying goodbye to Tane, interrupted him: 'She's going the other way—underground, I expect,' she said quickly. She nodded briefly to Euphemia. 'Bye,' she said, and got into the car at the kerb.

When it was out of sight Euphemia picked up her bag. 'I'll be off,' she said cheerfully. 'Thank you for having me to stay in Holland, I enjoyed it. I hope you have a good trip back tomorrow.'

Her bag was taken from her. 'A bit hasty, aren't you? Ah, here's the car—I'll drive you back to Hampton-cum-Spyway.'

'Whose car?'

'The one I arranged to hire until tomorrow.' His voice was patient as though she were an unwilling child, needing to be coaxed.

'But you've got an appointment—you said so.'

'Not until eight o'clock; it's only just turned four o'clock. I was hoping you'd invite me to tea.'

Euphemia watched the porter putting their cases in the boot and decided that there was nothing she could do about it. 'Well, of course I will. They'll all be home, so it'll be noisy.'

She got in beside him, feeling guilty because it should have been Diana sitting there, not she, and it would have been easier to have wished him goodbye at the airport and started to forget him then. Now she would be with him for at least another two hours. Her heart sang at the very idea.

They talked comfortably as they drove and Euphemia marvelled at the fact that she was so completely at ease with him. When she had first discovered that she loved him, she had dreaded having to see him again, but it hadn't been like that at all. She hadn't felt shy or awkward with him, only perfectly happy. She supposed Diana felt like that too, only she didn't show it.

She said out loud: 'I'm not very reserved, am I?' and at his startled look: 'I say things without thinking first and I do things on the spur of the moment...'

He said slowly on a laugh: 'Well, I can remember occasions—your urgent desire that I should choke on your cakes, being handed an apple core in the middle of a party, being told in no uncertain terms that I was a cold-blooded man...'

Euphemia said soberly: 'I'm sorry I said that—you see what I mean?'

'Indeed I do. Your company is nothing if not stimulating, Euphemia,' he glanced sideways at her, 'but a little dimmed of late, I fancy.'

'Yes—well, I expect that's because I was in another country.'

He looked as though he was going to laugh again. He said gravely: 'I expect it was. Presumably you will quickly become your old self once you're back on the ward.'

Cold comfort, though perhaps once she got back to the hospital, back into the routine and the never ending jobs, she would be able to take up life where she had left off, rub him out, as it were, as though he had never been. And that wouldn't work either, she reminded herself, for occasionally she would have to see him when he came on to the ward—she would have to fiddle the off-dutys so as not to be there... She frowned and he asked: 'Now what are you fussing about?'

'I'm not fussing.' She saw with relief that they were almost there; the first few cottages were already in sight, a minute later they were going slowly round the green and then in at the open gate. She was home, and so, she thought belatedly, was he.

They had been seen. The door was flung open and the boys rushed out followed by Ellen, who hugged Euphemia and then put up her face to be kissed by the doctor in the most natural way possible. 'I'm so glad you could come,' she told him. 'I've made a cake and Mrs Cross has cut mountains of sandwiches.'

Euphemia, listening with one ear to the boys' outpourings, thought it sounded as though Ellen had expected the doctor, but she was borne inside the house by her brothers, still talking, so that she forgot about it.

Nothing had been changed indoors, although she saw at once that the hole in the carpet had been beautifully mended. But there were flowers everywhere, the furniture shone and all the doors and windows were wide open. She cried happily: 'Oh, it's so good to be home!' and then felt awful because if the doctor had heard, he must have felt dreadfully uncomfortable. Apparently he hadn't. He was talking easily to Ellen, very much at home. But then why shouldn't he be? He lived there now.

They had tea in the dining-room, a substantial old-fashioned meal with plates of Mrs Cross's sandwiches, scones and jam, fruit cake and little iced buns, and Euphemia, behind the tea tray, busy filling teacups, sighed happily and when Ellen asked: 'Was it lovely at Jerez, Phemie? Were there lots of servants and gorgeous food?' she answered quickly: 'I'd rather be here. The servants were super, but Mrs Kellard dieted…'

There was a howl of laughter from the boys. 'Poor old Phemie—were you hungry all the time?'

'Yes, I think I was, though I expect it did me a lot of good. Don't I look any thinner?'

Everyone stared at her and Billy appealed to the doctor, who was staring as hard as the rest of them. 'She hasn't changed at all,' he said slowly, 'although she has got a nice tan on her.' He smiled at her across the table. 'It will show off your uniform nicely.'

She frowned a little, because she didn't want to be reminded of work—not just yet. 'It will wear off then,' she said shortly. 'Who wants more tea?'

The doctor had left a little later. Euphemia, watching his departure from the open door, thought peevishly that he might have been a much-loved uncle or old family friend, the way he was being sped on his way, what with Ellen hugging him with such warmth and the boys crowding round him like two affectionate puppies. And he could at least have waved as he drove off—but he hadn't even glanced in her direction.

CHAPTER EIGHT

THE WEEK which followed was sheer delight to Euphemia. Not wanting to waste a second of it, she was up early each morning to potter in the garden and tidy the house before breakfast so that the day was free to spend as they all wished. They visited old friends, had them to tea, played endless games of croquet on the lawn behind the house and when the mood took them, bundled into Euphemia's car and trundled away for a picnic. She would have liked it to last for ever. In her old home, doing all the things she enjoyed doing, she felt cocooned against her worries, and it was easier, though not impossible, to forget Tane and a future which held very little prospect of happiness.

She sat up late on her last night, after everyone else had gone to bed, wishing fruitlessly that things could be different, and because she couldn't sleep she went round the house, dusting and polishing soundlessly, which was a silly waste of time, because Mrs Cross was coming in in the morning after they had all gone to do just that ready for the doctor's return. And when that was precisely, Euphemia didn't know. He would be back in England by now, probably staying with Diana's family, but he came and went so often there was no knowing.

The boys went first. She drove them to the station and saw them on to their train with the promise that they would all meet at Aunt Thea's for half term, and by the time she got back Ellen's curate had arrived to drive her back to Middle Wallop. They had coffee together and she saw the pair of them off in the elderly Mini, sure in her own mind that they would be engaged before Christmas. At least Ellen was happy. The girl, so shy and awkward before, had blossomed into a young woman who would be quite capable of running a home. There would never be much money, of course, but Euphemia didn't think that mattered.

She went indoors then to have a few words with Mrs Cross before fetching her case and putting it in the boot and driving off back to work. London would be horrible, she thought, getting a last glimpse of the roses, still growing in profusion round the house.

The contrast certainly was cruel. St Cyprian's looked gloomier than ever and the mean little streets which surrounded its bulk seemed meaner than ever. The warm sunshine which should have made it look better only served to offer a cruel contrast to the quiet countryside she had just left. She went as usual to the parking place behind the hospital and got out, unable to stop herself looking round to see if the Bentley was there. It wasn't, and she stifled disappointment while at the same time telling herself that it was no concern of hers if it were.

It was mid-afternoon by now and the Nurses' Home was quiet. Euphemia unpacked slowly, arranged her small possessions round the room and went along to the Sisters' sitting-room for tea. They were all there, her friends, and she spent the next hour answering their questions about her trip, making it lighthearted and glossing over the duller bits.

'You've got a gorgeous tan,' said Laura Jeffs, the Relief Sister who had taken Euphemia's ward for her while she was away. 'It'll do the patients good just to look at you. Did you sunbathe every day and all day?'

'Well, not quite, but a good deal of the time. How's the ward?'

They talked shop after that until some of them, those of them who hadn't already gone back on duty, wandered off to get ready for an evening out with boy-friends or family. Euphemia, left with one or two of the older Sisters earnestly discussing the treatment of diabetes, picked up the paper and began to read it without a word. She supposed that given another ten years or so, she would be like her companions, and the idea appalled her.

There were a lot of new faces amongst her patients when she went on duty the next morning, but Dicky and Mr Crouch were still there and they welcomed her each in his own way, Mr Crouch with a few snarling grumbles and Dicky with a wide smile and a garbled flood of words expressing his pleasure at seeing her again. Euphemia went round the ward, taking her time, getting to know the occupants of the beds. There were a lot of elderly men this time, heart conditions, chest conditions—most of them should have been in hospital weeks earlier, but she guessed that they had hung on, hoping they would get better without going to the doctor. Jobs were hard to come by these days and those that had them wanted to keep them.

Joan Willis, giving her a detailed report later, advised her that several of them were considered to be very poorly by Sir Richard Blake. 'He said,' observed her loyal right hand, 'that he was glad you were coming back because then they'd have a good chance.'

Euphemia, who had been feeling low-spirited, perked up a little. Challenge and hard work—there was nothing like them to take one's mind off other things.

For the first few days she went on duty warily, expecting to see Tane coming on to the ward, but Sir Richard's round came and went and there was no sign of him. Illogically, that upset her; she had wanted never to see him again, but he could at least have enquired as to whether she had settled back to work. She was even more upset to discover from Joan when she returned from her off duty a week after her return that he had been on the ward in her absence; had stayed for more that half an hour, in fact, and had then accepted a cup of tea from her staff nurse.

Joan, seeing the look on Euphemia's face, had added doubtfully: 'I hope you don't mind—he was so friendly…'

'Mind? Why should I mind?' snapped Euphemia, her cheeks pink and her tawny eyes glowing with ill humour. 'He can drink all the tea he wants as far as I'm concerned. What did he say about Mr Duke?'

Mr Duke was elderly, irascible, and desperately ill with a virus infection of the chest which refused to respond to antibiotics.

Nothing more had been said about Dr van Diederijk and he wasn't on Sir Richard's round the next day, so it was all the more vexing to hear at midday dinner that he had been to the women's medical ward that morning. 'He said he'd be coming to see you tomorrow morning,' remarked Doreen Marks, Sister on that ward. 'You've got some pretty poorly men, haven't you?'

Euphemia replied suitably while she mentally read-justed the off-duty for the next day. She had arranged to have her two days off at the end of the week and Joan hadn't minded when she had hers. She swallowed the rest of her dinner, declared that she had so much to do she wouldn't have her usual cup of tea with the others, and flew back to her office. Joan was there, waiting for her return, and Euphemia lost no time in putting her plan into operation.

'Joan, would it bother you if I took my days off tomorrow and Thursday? You could have Friday and Saturday—I particularly want to go down to see Ellen.'

Joan gave her a sympathetic look. Poor old Euphemia must be having a pretty rotten time of it since her father died. 'I don't mind a bit—in fact I'd love to have those two days. I can go shopping when Mother comes up to town.'

'Bless you!' Euphemia beamed at her. 'Go to your dinner, will you, and take Nurse Simmons and Nurse Collins with you, then when you get back we'll go through the report together.'

She was to have been off duty that evening anyway. By six o'clock she was edging the Morris out of the hospital courtyard, a hastily packed bag on the seat behind her. There hadn't been much time; she had had to telephone the office about the change of duty and do one or two ward chores she wouldn't have done until later on in the week, but she had had time to shower and change into a jumper and skirt and fling a blazer into the back seat to join the bag. There was a lot of traffic; it took a bit of manoeuvring to get into the busy street outside and she didn't see the doctor's Bentley nose past into the hospital forecourt. She didn't see the surprise on his face either, nor the slow smile which followed it.

She was at Sunbury turning on to the M3 when she remembered that she hadn't telephoned Aunt Thea. Not that that goodnatured lady would mind; although Euphemia had told Ellen before she went back that she wouldn't be going down to Middle Wallop for a month and Ellen would have passed that on to her aunt.

It was a fine evening and the motorway was fairly empty. The days were beginning to draw in, and when she stopped for petrol she felt a faint nip in the air—summer would soon be over, before long she would have to think about Christmas and the holidays. There would be no hope of them being together this year; she would be on duty, but perhaps Aunt Thea would have the boys as well as Ellen, but Aunt Thea wasn't young any more and Euphemia didn't think any of her other relations would invite them to stay. She thrust the problem aside and concentrated on her driving.

Aunt Thea and Ellen were washing up their supper dishes when she opened the front door of the cottage, but they left them at once, carried her off into the sitting room with the promise of something to eat immediately and demanded to know why she was there. 'Not but what you're more than welcome,' declared Aunt Thea, 'but you usually telephone…'

'Well, I had to change my days off at a moment's notice,' Euphemia explained, 'and I just wanted to come— I do hope you don't mind?'

'Of course not, love—you know how pleased we are to see you. Just you sit there with Ellen while I get your supper.' The dear soul bustled out of the room and Ellen asked:

'Is it awful being back, Phemie? You must miss that lovely villa.'

'I miss Myrtle House more,' said Euphemia. 'Don't you?'

Ellen smiled. 'Oh yes—but it's nice here.'

'How is the curate?'

Ellen blushed. 'Why do you call him the curate, like that? His name's Tom. He's very well. We're going to Salisbury tomorrow—it's his day off. Would you like to come with us?'

Euphemia smiled at her sister. 'No, thank you, darling—I'd like to potter about here. I've had a busy week.'

'Poor Phemie. Have you seen Tane?'

Euphemia was taking off her shoes and wiggling her toes in comfort.

'No—he came to the ward when I was off duty.'

'What a shame! He's such a dear, and so easy to talk to—like a brother.'

Euphemia threw a quick glance at her sister. Ellen was a guileless girl, but had that remark been quite as innocent as it sounded? She decided it had. 'He and Diana are getting married soon, I believe,' she said.

'I can't think why,' said Ellen.

A remark Euphemia heartily endorsed.

The cottage was blissfully quiet after St Cyprian's. She slept like a top and spent the day as she had promised herself, pottering, mostly in the garden, weeding and tidying up and then helping her aunt indoors while she regaled that lady with the more lighthearted events of her stay at Jerez. Ellen and Tom had left quite early in the morning and it was well after teatime when they got back, looking so pleased with themselves that Euphemia and her aunt, taking their ease in the small front garden, got to their feet and went to meet them, the answer to their unspoken question so obvious that they didn't need to ask it.

'We're engaged!' cried Ellen, and flung herself at the pair of them in turn, triggering off a round of congratulations, hand-shakings and excited talk until Aunt Thea declared that the occasion merited a glass of the sherry she had been hoarding for a special occasion. And there was a supper party presently, with Aunt Thea and Euphemia in the kitchen beating eggs and whipping cream and arranging a magnificent salad.

They would marry next year, said Tom, and within a short time he hoped to get a parish of his own, and would Aunt Thea mind if Ellen married from her house? The evening passed in a flash and later, when Ellen had walked over with Tom to see the Rector, Euphemia had persuaded her aunt to go to bed while she washed the supper things. It was wonderful news, she told herself, and exactly what she had hoped for. Ellen was a darling and Tom was quite right for her; calm, patient and reassuring.

Euphemia heaved an enormous sigh and went to bed. She loved her sister too much to be envious of her, but she couldn't help wondering how it would feel to be engaged to Tane; a useless piece of thinking which would get her nowhere, but it made sleeping for a good deal of the night, at any rate, an impossibility.

It was a beautiful morning again. Euphemia, up and

about early, got breakfast for them all, waved goodbye to Ellen, off to spend the morning with her elderly employer, flew round the cottage doing the small household chores and then went into the garden. There were several apple trees in the rough bit at the bottom and a plum tree or two. She picked plums for her aunt's jam-making and then went to look at the apples. Most of them had good crops, but not quite ready for picking. There was one elderly tree— Scarlet Pimpernel—whose fruit hung ready to be eaten. Euphemia chose an apple, rubbed it up on the sleeve of her blouse, and sat down to eat it. She was munching contentedly when she heard footsteps coming down the brick path from the back door, and looked up to see Tane coming towards her. Happiness flooded her so completely that she couldn't speak, so she went on chewing, looking at every loved inch of him, longing to tell him that she loved him more than anything else in her world.

He came to a halt a foot or so away and stood looking down at her.

'You really are a girl for apples, aren't you? Can it be pure chance or are you tempting me?'

She swallowed her mouthful. 'I didn't know you were coming, and even if I did, I wouldn't.'

He picked an apple from the tree and sat down beside her.

'You're not dressed for the country,' observed Euphemia, taking in the clerical grey, the silk tie, the beautifully polished shoes.

'I'm on my way to Bristol—there's a seminar there. I could hardly attend it in slacks and a sweater and there'll be no time to change if I'm staying for lunch.'

She leant up on an elbow the better to look at him. 'Have you been invited, or are you just hoping you will be?'

'I've been invited—your aunt and I get on very well together.' He threw away the core and lay back against the tree. 'How's the ward?'

'Busy, you know that.' Euphemia paused and then asked in a rush: 'How's Diana?'

'Oh, very much better for her rest. And you? Are you very much better, Euphemia?'

'I've not been ill…'

'Who said that you had?' His voice was as bland as his face.

She got to her feet, fearful of being asked more questions. 'I expect you'd like coffee—I'll make some.'

He had got up too. 'Your aunt put the kettle on when I got here. Euphemia, are you happy?'

She had snatched up her basket of plums. 'Yes, of course I am. What a silly question!'

'No sillier than your answer.' His voice was silky and she sensed more probings and questions.

'Well, we'd better go and have our coffee,' she said quickly. 'I daresay you want to leave directly after lunch.'

He took her basket from her. 'Of course, if you do not wish me to stay to lunch…' His voice was silkier than ever.

'Oh, of course not—it's quite immaterial to me. Aunt Thea loves having people…'

'And you don't—or is it just me?' He was laughing at her now, and suddenly she found herself laughing too.

Ellen brought Tom back for lunch and the whole meal

was taken up with plans for the wedding, most of them lighthearted. Euphemia found herself wondering if Tane and Diana had as much fun planning theirs, and thought it unlikely.

Tane left soon after lunch, with a great hug and kiss for Aunt Thea, who blushed rosily and declared that he'd do better to kiss someone nearer his own age, whereupon he kissed Ellen and then, with an absentminded air, Euphemia.

'Nice chap,' declared Tom, watching the Bentley slide away into the village. Aunt Thea and Ellen agreed wholeheartedly, but Euphemia said nothing at all.

She went back to St Cyprian's the next morning, very early so that she could go on duty after midday dinner. The ward was just as busy and the ill patients just as ill. She spent the afternoon arranging X-rays, test meals, ECGs and blood transfusions for two new patients with duodenal ulcers. Terry Walker had been on the ward for most of the time; it amused her in a wry fashion to see how his manner had subtly changed towards her. She had never taken his proposals seriously, but now he was being very careful to let her see that he hadn't been serious either; he was friendly enough but wary with it. It didn't matter in the least to her, but her pride was hurt; she had thought that he liked her for herself and not for her prospects, and now that she had none, she wondered if he had ever had any real feelings for her at all. Probably not.

She missed tea, swallowed a cup on the ward and didn't go off duty until the night staff were on, which was just as well, because she was in no mood to exchange gossip with her friends before going to bed. She ate a solitary supper in the canteen and went straight to bed, feeling bad-tempered. She knew why, of course; Tane was in Bristol and probably she wouldn't see him for days, perhaps weeks. She had given up her resolve to avoid him, forget him even, for she was powerless to do that; he was there all the time at the back of her head. She supposed that he would fade slowly; she supposed too that if she found another job a long way away so that she had no chance of seeing him at all, he might fade a good deal faster. She lay in bed toying with the idea of going somewhere really remote like Tristan da Cunha and fell asleep in the middle of her planning.

She had been back four days when the letter came. She had been in her office, making up the books, puzzling over the off duty and checking the charts. She had almost finished when Willis put her head round the door. 'Post for you, Sister, it's just come up.' She laid a long envelope on the desk and slipped away, and Euphemia laid aside the chart she was writing up and reached for it. It was from Messrs Fish, Fish and Thrums, Solicitors, and she wondered what Mr Fish could be writing about now. The sorry business of small debts; official papers and funeral expenses had all been dealt with, the rent from the house was being paid in regularly and the mortgage payments were arranged; as far as she knew, there was nothing more than needed her attention.

She was wrong. She read the rather long letter through, going pale as she did so, her frown thunderous. Having read it, she smoothed it out on the desk before her and read it again, slowly this time. The contents remained the same; Dr van Diederijk's solicitor had written to inform Mr Fish that his client had taken over the mortgage of Myrtle House and in future all repayments should be made to him on behalf of the doctor.

'But he can't!' She didn't know that she had spoken out loud. 'He simply can't—and why should he?' She began to read the letter for the third time, to be interrupted by her staff nurse once more, this time with an urgent request for her to come into the ward immediately and take a look at Mr Cummins, who was, unless her faithful right hand was mistaken, on the verge of another coronary.

There was no time to do anything about the letter for that day. Mr Cummins and his coronary kept them all busy, as did the rest of the ward, and by the time she got off duty, Euphemia saw to her dismay that it was long past the time for any self-respecting solicitor to be in his office. It would have to wait till the morning. She spent a wretched night and went on duty looking far from her best, and feeling even worse.

Surprisingly and fortunately, the ward had quietened down considerably—not that she had any false hopes about that; the ill men were still very ill and any one of them might spring a surprise without warning. But just for the moment the ward routine went smoothly ahead and presently she was able to go to the office and tackle the paper work. She was filling in a requisition form for more bed linen when the door opened and the doctor walked in. Euphemia put down her pen slowly, horrified that her mouth was trembling, fighting to preserve a calm front. She even managed a normal-sounding 'Good morning, Doctor,' in reply to his civil greeting and then sat waiting for him to speak, wishing that he wasn't quite such a big man, towering over her in the little room.

'You had a letter about the mortgage?' he wanted to know.

'Yes.'

'Good. Perhaps I should have mentioned it when I saw you last, but it seemed better that it should be settled by our solicitors. It makes no difference to you.'

Her numbed thoughts came to life then. Colour flushed her cheeks and her eyes glowed with topaz light. 'What do you mean by that? Of course it makes a difference to me— instead of paying some man I've never even met, I have to pay you, and supposing I can't pay? Supposing I can't find another tenant when you go? You can foreclose. That's what you want to do, isn't it?' She was furious now, the words tumbling out. 'I suppose Diana decided that she'd like to live there for always and you thought this up between you? Pretending to be a—a friend and worming your way into everyone's good graces! I imagine that's why you wanted me to go to Jerez with Diana, so that I'd be out of the way while you arranged it all.'

She would have liked to have screamed at him, but that wouldn't do, so close to the ward, and people going too and fro. 'How dared you?' she said in a stony voice, and stopped because she had run out of breath. Before she could begin again, Tane leaned over the desk and took her hands in his. 'Euphemia, listen.'

She tugged uselessly. 'No, I won't! I know what you're going to say and I don't want to see you or speak to you ever again! I'll have to, of course, when you're on the ward, but I'll not utter one word unless it's about the patients.' She gave another tug at her hands and his grip tightened just a little. 'Let go,' she flared at him, 'or I'll scream!'

He laughed softly. 'You're very angry, aren't you, Phemie? But that's because you're jumping to conclusions—women do.'

'Don't be pompous,' she snapped. 'Be good enough to let me go and go away.' She forced herself to look at him and added quietly: 'I mean that.'

He straightened up slowly and released her hands. There was no hint of anger in his face, but she sat back rather quickly, away from him. He said coldly: 'If you want it that way—and you don't have to duck away like that, I'm not going to hit you.' His eyes were as cold as his voice, but, 'I should like to shake you until your teeth rattle, Sister Blackstock.'

He went unhurriedly to the door. 'Just remember one thing, will you? I'm a man of infinite patience when I want something.' He closed the door very quietly behind him.

'And what does he mean by that?' muttered Euphemia distractedly. 'He's got what he wants. Oh, I hate him, I hate him!' She picked up Mr Fish's letter with a hand that shook and folded it neatly and put it in her pocket. She would have to write to him, she supposed, or better still go and see him. Regardless of hospital rules, she telephoned for an appointment then and there. 'Two o'clock,' said an elderly female voice at the other end of the line. 'Mr Fish could spare ten minutes or so.'

Mr Fish's office wasn't so very far away, Lincoln's Inn, but Euphemia, changing her off duty to a split and going to second dinner, had to miss her meal in order to get there on time. And her temper was hardly improved to find that when she got there that Mr Fish was engaged, so that she had to sit in a bare little waiting room, leafing through vintage copies of *The Field,* quite unable to think up any planned speeches. It was partly hunger, of course; she had had a cup of tea and half a slice of toast at breakfast and she'd been too upset to do more than sip her coffee during the morning. Now her insides rumbled emptily, taking her mind off the matter in hand. And at the back of it all was the ruthlessly flattened down image of Tane. By the time she got into Mr Fish's stuffy office she hadn't a coherent thought left in her head.

But not so Mr Fish. After all, he got his living by being coherent; he listened in a fatherly way to her protests and then tore them to shreds with a few well chosen sentences. What did it matter, he pointed out kindly, who held the mortgage? Indeed, he considered that Dr van Diederijk was a much sounder proposition than the small private firm who had taken up the mortgage in the first place and why, he added as an aside, her father had not gone to a reputable building society or even the bank, he couldn't understand. He could not see what difference it could possibly make to her. He chuckled to himself for a moment. 'And you do realise that the doctor is being paid back with his own money, my dear? At least until he gives up the tenancy of Myrtle House.'

'Yes, but when he does, don't you see, Mr Fish? If I can't find another tenant at once I can't repay the mortgage, then he can take the house away from us—it'll be his!'

Mr Fish sat back and patted his fingertips together in a way that got on her stretched nerves. 'Oh, I don't think so, my dear. He is, I understand, in no need of financial aid, he could well afford to wait until such time as a new tenant was found. But are you not crossing your bridges before you reach them? Supposing you leave everything to me. Your dear father seldom took my advice, but I hope that you will.'

Euphemia left it at that. Mr Fish looked mild and elderly and incapable of saying boo to a goose, but he had floored her with his dry, logical talk. She wished him a polite good day and took herself off, got a bus to Oxford Street and had a highly indigestible tea in one of the more expensive cafés. It was the sort of thing she seldom did, but she felt defiant and dreadfully unhappy as well as hungry.

The afternoon's visit to Mr Fish had been a complete waste of time, she decided as she changed back into uniform, and as far as she could see there was nothing more to be done, and since she had made it clear that she didn't want anything to do with Tane ever again, she couldn't discuss it further with him. Anyway, he wouldn't listen. 'Arrogant, pigheaded man!' cried Euphemia, ramming her cap on to her dark piled-up hair.

There was enough work on the ward to keep her mind occupied until she went off duty that evening—more than enough, she thought worriedly: three of her patients were very poorly and Terry had been in and out several times to see them, and the various treatments he ordered kept her and the nurses busy until the night staff came on duty. Even then, she didn't hurry off duty but went to her supper late, then went along to the Sisters' sitting-room to drink tea and talk shop. It was much later than usual by the time she got to bed and she was so tired that she slept at once.

It was Sir Richard's round in the morning, and Euphemia heaved a sigh of relief when she saw that he was on his own. She had tried not to think about meeting Tane on the ward and the longer it could be put off the better. The round took a long time, with Sir Richard being nastier than ever to the students dogging his footsteps and wanting treatments changed and impossibilities like instant X-rays. Euphemia edged him slowly from bed to bed while two nurses followed discreetly at a distance, restoring the chaos of tossed bedclothes, scattered notes and written requests for barium meals, blood tests, physiotherapy and the like. It was almost noon by the time he stalked into her office, to be calmed with coffee and biscuits. 'A pity van Diederijk was called back to Holland for some consultation or other,' he grumbled to her. 'I should have liked to have consulted with him myself. That man—what's his name, third bed on the right… Cummins, is it? His general condition isn't good…' He launched into technicalities, and Euphemia made herself concentrate on what he was saying and tried not to wonder why Tane should have gone back to Holland so very suddenly. It must have been something very urgent—or was it an excuse so that they shouldn't meet for a little while? Perhaps he had thought that she would be more amenable if he left her alone for a while? Nothing, she decided hotly, would make her that.

'Sister…' Sir Richard, his voice raised, had obviously been waiting for her to say something, but she had no idea what it was. She apologised and bent her mind to the problem as to whether Mr Drew should have his insulin increased or not. On her own at last, she sorted notes and tidied away charts, had a quick consultation with Joan and went to her dinner.

'Late again,' observed the occupants of her table.

'Sir Richard,' Euphemia murmured, and made a face. 'An hour and a half, and I've lost count of the forms to be filled in…it's not my day!'

And as it turned out it wasn't. Visitors came and went, and all but one student nurse had gone to tea, leaving Euphemia to deal with drips and the inhalations Sir Richard approved of for his chest cases, while the nurses tidied lockers and beds and bore away the unsuitable food and sweets which the visitors always brought with them despite Euphemia's patient explanations as to what exactly the patients were allowed. The nurse had just left the ward, her arms full of the diabetic's toffees, the duodenal ulcer's iced buns and the bunch of bananas given to a nasty case of colitis, when there was a loud rumbling which became a roar of sound as one side of the ward seemed to shake and quiver and become submerged in a cloud of dust and broken glass and falling plaster.

CHAPTER NINE

EUPHEMIA, BENDING OVER Mr Cummins, clutched the edge of the bed to prevent herself falling. Something catastrophic had happened, but for a few seconds her shocked brain didn't react, then common sense, training and a naturally calm disposition took over. She gave Mr Cummins' grey face a reassuring smile and took stock of the ward. The opposite wall had taken the full force of the explosion, so it must have been outside in the street below and although the wall still stood, it was cracked and sagging and the plaster was dropping in great chunks off it. The windows had been blown out and there was glass everywhere. Luckily it had fallen in the centre of the ward and missed the beds and their occupants, but not all of them. Euphemia could hear shouts and moans above the general din now, and some of the up patients were staggering around in a dazed manner.

The inner wall seemed solid enough at the moment. There were no windows on that side, and the floor seemed solid too. She wasn't so sure about the centre, though, but she would have to risk that. 'Everyone stay where he is!' she shouted at the top of her voice. 'There'll be help in a moment, so don't worry.' The absurdity of her words struck her as she uttered them; she was worried stiff and terrified too. Supposing the outside wall collapsed—or the floor? It didn't bear thinking of, so she didn't, but edged her way cautiously from bed to bed making sure that each patient was at least alive. They were, some of them only just, but it was no time for intensive care it was imperative for her to get to the other side where the moans were getting louder. She went to the end of the ward and started to cross the floor gingerly as near the end wall as possible. When she reached the ruined door she saw the student nurse picking herself up off the landing floor. She waved gamely when she saw Euphemia and started towards her.

'Oh, good girl!' cried Euphemia. Nurse Shotter wasn't quick or particularly clever, but she loved her work and now she was showing pluck when she might so easily have been indulging in a screaming fit. 'Come carefully, the floor's not too safe.' She put out a hand and steadied the girl into the ward. 'There'll be help presently, but I don't think we'd better wait for it. Will you go very carefully down the inner wall and lead out all the men who can possibly walk? I can see the stairs—they'll be the safest place, I should think. Sit them down on the treads, then they can be got away when we get help.' She gave the girl's arm a reassuring squeeze. 'But go carefully, for heaven's sake. I'll be on the outer side—on no account are you to come there, and if anyone comes warn them not to come over until someone lets us know if the floors are safe.'

'But, Sister...'

'Off you go, Shotter.'

Euphemia watched her make her careful way to the

first bed. Dicky was in it; he looked scared, but as always
he did as he was told. He began to get carefully out of bed
under Shotter's guidance, and Euphemia turned away and
started for the first bed on the other side. The dust was sub-
siding now, leaving the beds thick with it, their occupants
too. Testing the floor at each step, she made her way slowly
from bed to bed, wiping faces, looking for injuries, reassuring them with a cheerfulness which sounded hollow in
her own ears and must have sounded even more so in
theirs. The two top beds held men who could walk if they
had to. Euphemia guided them, one at a time, keeping
close to the beds, listening to the ominous creaks from the
floor beneath them. That left ten men to move. Six of them
just couldn't walk, the others oughtn't to, but they'd have
to. She paused for a moment to look across to the other side
and saw that Shotter had got four men away already and
at the same time became aware of the noise going on
around her—shouts and cries and every now and then, the
sound of bricks tumbling. She wondered what the damage
was outside and below them and remembered with thank-
fulness that it was the OP Department and the early afternoon clinic would be finished.

She could hear sirens wailing now and someone out in
the street giving orders. It wouldn't be long before they got
help now, in the meantime she had better move some more
patients. She still wasn't happy about the floor, and if it gave
way it would be difficult to get the men out of the beds
farthest away from the door. That made Mr Crouch next.
Mr Crouch had a great many reasons for not getting out of
his bed and making the journey to the door. Euphemia
listened patiently to them all while she dragged on his

dressing gown and slippers, swung his protesting legs out of his bed and urged him past the other beds. He disputed every inch of the way and she was a nervous wreck by the time they reached the landing where Nurse Shotter took him over.

It was on the way back to the end of the ward that Euphemia felt the floor beneath her shudder. There was a nasty cracking sound too, and she stood still, too frightened to move. But nothing happened and presently she crept on again, intent on reaching Mr Cummins, who was looking almost unconscious. A small surge of sound and low voices made her stop and look round. There were men at the door—policemen, firemen, hospital porters standing in a bunch listening to Tane, towering above them, his jacket off, his hair colourless with dust. Euphemia's heart gave a great leap so that she lost her breath and her voice came out in a high squeak. 'Don't come along this side,' she called, 'the floor's beginning to move!'

They all looked at her, calling out heartening remarks like: 'Hold on, Sister', and 'You're OK now', but Tane didn't say a word, only muttered something to the men and started towards her.

'Don't—don't come,' cried Euphemia, 'the floor's going to give and you're far too heavy!'

She heard him laugh and then watched while he came slowly up the ward. When he reached her he said: 'Hullo—they're getting the fire escapes into position, we can get them out through the windows. It won't take long.' He smiled at her. It was a nice smile, full of confidence and cheerfulness and tenderness too. She discovered that she wasn't afraid any more and said in a voice which shook only a very little: 'Mr Cummins isn't very well—could you look at him? The others aren't too bad, but some of them have got cuts from the glass…'

She had a cut herself, although she hadn't noticed it. She had lost her cap too and her hair was a fearful tangle of dust and plaster, its pins lost, so that it hung in matted clusters round her head. She was white under her dirty face too and her hands shook a little as she turned down the tumbled bedclothes so that the doctor could take a look at Mr Cummins.

The doctor bent calmly over the bed, seemingly unaware of the creaks and rumbles going on around him. There wasn't much he could do, but Mr Cummins, opening his eyes to see a doctor bending over him, took heart and began to breathe properly once more, happily not altogether aware of what was happening around him. He whispered: 'That was a bit of a bang,' and nodded, quite satisfied, when the doctor said calmly: 'A gas main in the street outside: it's being dealt with now and there's nothing for you to worry about. We'll have you out of here and in a clean bed in no time.'

The man in the next bed had a cut arm. The doctor examined it briefly and said: 'Tear up a sheet and bind it fairly tightly, it'll hold until we can get it seen to.' He turned his back on Euphemia and began a careful journey back towards the door, to meet the two men waiting by the end bed. They had a light stretcher with them and the three of them lifted its occupant on to it and the two men began their slow progress to the door. Euphemia, ready with her first aid, tore up another length of sheet. There was a man two beds down the ward with a small head wound, she might as well bind it…

'Stay where you are,' called Tane sharply, 'and keep still!' The floor heaved slowly as he spoke and she watched with fascinated horror as its centre slowly caved in and sent a shower of cement and wooden flooring on to the rubble below. There were still a couple of feet beyond the ends of the beds. She wondered how long it would be before that broke away too, although the inner wall of the ward was still holding and the floor comparatively solid on that side. And as though she wasn't scared enough she had to stand and watch the doctor making his way along the ruined edge of the floor. He did it unhurriedly and with a monumental calm, and when he reached her finally she couldn't detect even the smallest quickening of his breath. He didn't speak to her but edged past towards one of the shattered windows behind Mr Cummins' bed. A moment later she knew why; the first of the fire escapes had arrived.

'You will do exactly as I say,' said Tane, 'and you are not to move unless I tell you to,' an order she was only too glad to obey. She discontinued Mr Cummins' drip, miraculously still in position, folded back the bedclothes, covered him with a blanket and stood, hardly daring to breathe while Tane bent over the bed, picked up the old man and passed him through the window to the fireman waiting at the top of the escape. It seemed unlikely that he would survive the journey to the ground, but at least he had a chance. The escape disappeared from view and Tane leaned back over the empty bed, picked her up and set her gently down close to the next bed.

It was Mr Duke's turn. He had no drip, but Euphemia did as she was told—rolled back the bedclothes, tucked a blanket round him and waited while Tane picked him up and edged him through the window behind the bed into the arms of the firemen on the second fire escape. It took a good deal longer this time, because Mr Duke was a long thin man and difficult to manoeuvre, and Euphemia, watching, longed to express her feelings with a good scream. She did in fact let out a whispered shriek during the next fifteen minutes, for after the next man had been got away and she was wrapping a blanket round the very last patient, the floor's rumblings became louder and a great deal more of it went the way of the rest, carrying part of the end wall with it, which left them standing on a kind of sagging shelf under the windows, the row of beds still there, battered and awry.

Euphemia, who had never fainted in her life, thought how nice it would be if she could now and come to safely on the ground. The patient was semi-conscious and unco-operative, and it seemed to her that Tane would never get him through the window. But he did, and that left the two of them with the second fire escape already on its way up. Euphemia gave a gusty sigh and managed a smile. It lasted barely a second, for there was another cracking and tearing and the end bed began to slide slowly over the edge of the floor and toppled over in a kind of slow motion into the mess below. 'Oh,' said Euphemia, 'look—they'll all go!' She cast a despairing glance at Tane and was annoyed to see him looking quite calm. 'I'm frightened,' she snapped in a quaking voice. 'Aren't you?'

'Terrified. Let's get up into this window, we can hold on to the wall.'

'There won't be a wall,' she wailed, and then said: 'Sorry,' in a voice rigid with fear but under control again.

Tane went first, testing the rubble round the broken window, and pulled her up after him. There wasn't much room, but the wall, although damaged and heavily cracked, might stand even if the rest of the floor went. Which it did a few seconds later, leaving them with nothing but the wall to which they were clinging. Tane put an arm round her shoulders and tucked her head against his chest. His voice, very quiet and steady, calmed her even though it didn't stop her shaking. 'The escape is almost here,' he told her, 'and when it is you're going to be a brave girl and do exactly as you're told. Don't look down, just look at the fireman.'

'You're coming too? Tane, I won't go without you.'

'I'm coming too. Here we are—now, do exactly as I say…'

She thought at first that she wouldn't be able to do that; she was stiff with fright when she saw the gap she would have to cross to reach the escape—a very narrow gap, only a few inches, but supposing she slipped?

'Come along, darling,' said Tane briskly.

It was being called darling that did it. Euphemia leaned out, grasped the rail of the escape and was safely there with the fireman's steady arm round her, watching Tane doing the same thing. There didn't seem much room; the fireman was a big man too, but she was thankful to feel safely squashed between them, because she hated heights. She squeezed her eyes tight shut and without knowing it, clung to Tane's arm. Now that they were safe she felt dazed and very sick. She hardly realised the fact that they had reached the ground and the doctor, looking into her greenish white face, took her hands firmly from his sleeve and handed her over to the Senior Nursing Officer and Home Sister.

She was only just aware of being put into an ambulance and driven the short distance round the hospital to the Nurses' Home, undamaged by the blast, and she made almost no protest when she was undressed, bathed, her hair washed and popped into bed. She slept all night and, being young and strong, woke at her usual time in the morning, feeling none the worse for her experience. To Home Sister's agitated advice to return to her bed for the day she replied quite truthfully that she felt very well and that since she was, she would go on duty, because there must be a mass of work to do. She was greeted like a heroine at breakfast and there was such a lot to be told and listened to that no one remembered that the Senior Nursing Officer had accompanied Doctor van Diederijk over to the home late on the previous evening and paid her a visit. They had stood in her room, looking down at her sleeping face with its curtain of dark hair spread on the pillow, and the Senior Nursing Officer had murmured something appropriate about her being a brave young woman who had done her duty. She had expected the doctor to say something in like vein, or at least agree with her, but all he said was: 'Well, she looks fine to me. She'll be perfectly all right after a good night's sleep.'

The Senior Nursing Officer had been a little shocked by his indifference and then excused him because, after all, he was a foreigner and somewhat cold in his manner, even though his manners were perfect.

Euphemia found her patients temporarily housed in the physiotherapy department at the other end of the hospital, which had escaped lightly from the blast, having the whole of the centre of the vast building as well as the wing which had caught the full force of the explosion, between it and the burst gas main. The men were in hastily erected beds arranged haphazardly around the whole department, and although the ill ones were connected to their drips and monitors there was a woeful lack of simple equipment. Euphemia went round having a word with the men and then repaired to the tiny office where she gathered her nurses around her to be given a brief résumé of what had happened after she had left the scene.

There were cries of admiration for her conduct, of course, but she was a modest young woman and while she thanked them she pointed out that if any of them had been there they would have done exactly the same as she had done. 'And Nurse Shotter,' she observed, 'was very brave. We can all be proud of her.' Everyone looked at the student nurse, who went bright red and mumbled something. 'She could have turned tail and run for it, and I wouldn't have blamed her.' Euphemia beamed at the girl. 'What luck they came when they did or we should have been in the soup.'

'It's in all the papers,' said a voice. 'No one was hurt—not badly, anyway. Lucky it wasn't the rush hour.'

'What will happen to the ward, Sister?' asked Joan Willis. 'We can't stay here, can we?'

Euphemia shook her head. 'It's not very likely. I daresay I'll know more about that later on. I'll let you know when I do. Now let's get to work, there's an awful lot of stuff we simply must have right away—I'll make a list and see if I can get it at once. The men have recovered marvellously, but all the same I think I'll get Doctor Walker down to take a look at Mr Cummins.'

Terry came presently, pronounced Mr Cummins in a fair

condition, considering his experience, and after a look at the remainder of the patients followed her into the office. 'And you, Euphemia?' he wanted to know. 'Quite the little heroine and none the worse for it.'

She said seriously: 'Nothing like that. I couldn't do anything else, could I? I was scared stiff.'

'Dr van Diederijk was pretty cool too, everyone's singing his praises.' He added huffily: 'Just my luck to have had a half day—I should have done exactly what he did.'

'Of course,' agreed Euphemia kindly, and wondered what she had seen in Terry—and as for marrying him... She didn't want to think about marrying; there would never be another man to take Tane's place in her heart. She sighed and ordered coffee.

She was sent for during the morning to go to the Senior Nursing Officer's office. Miss Risby spent quite a time making a gracious speech concerning Euphemia's presence of mind, courage and good sense. Euphemia, acutely uncomfortable, sat on the edge of her chair and wished herself anywhere but there, but she knew Miss Risby of old, a formidable, well corseted lady with a sense of self-importance which had got her far in her profession. She endured the speech to its end, thanked Miss Risby politely and asked what plans had been made for her ward.

'Well now, Sister,' said Miss Risby, for once a little short of words, 'I've given the matter a good deal of thought and I've also been advised by Dr van Diderijk, whose judgement I value, especially as Sir Richard is on holiday. He suggests, most wisely, that we should transfer the patients from your ward to St Jude's—he has patients there, as you know—until such time as they can be accommodated here.'

'And when will that be, Miss Risby?' Euphemia's voice was very even.

'That's hard to say, Sister. As you can see for yourself, the damage to your wing is extensive; it will be necessary to erect some kind of a temporary ward to house the men's medical, and that will take some time—a few months, shall we say…'

'And my staff and myself?' asked Euphemia.

'Integrated into other wards. As for yourself, I suggest that you take the post of relief Sister until such time as the temporary building is ready.'

'Dr van Diederijk suggested that too, Miss Risby?'

'Indeed, yes. Such a resourceful man!'

Euphemia said nothing. He wasn't resourceful; he was arrogant, thoughtless and for some reason intent on messing up her life for her. Perhaps he was doing it to teach her a lesson because she had told him that she had hated him. She longed to give in her notice then and there, but she dared not—she had no job to go to and even a month without work would play havoc with her finances. All the same she would start looking around for another post and when she'd found one she'd let him know and he'd realise that she had no intention of dancing to his tune.

'Something is worrying you, Sister?' enquired Miss Risby.

Euphemia presented a blandly smiling face. 'No, Miss Risby, thank you. You will let me know when we are to be transferred? And am I to tell the nurses?'

'By all means—I should think the move might be managed within a week or ten days, that will fit in splendidly for you. Sister Thorn from Children's will be going on holiday then and you can take over from her.'

Euphemia stood up, received a gracious dismissal, and took herself off. If Dr van Diederijk had happened to have been at hand at that moment she would have boxed his ears for him. Probably it would have hurt her a good deal more than him, but it would have relieved her pent-up feelings.

She passed on Miss Risby's instructions when she returned to the ward, but there was precious little time to comment on them. The place was still in some disorder and they were all hard at it, setting it to rights, when the door was thrust open and Sir Richard came in and, with him, Dr van Diederijk.

Euphemia put down the pile of blankets she was distributing and advanced to meet them, to be greeted by Sir Richard at his heartiest.

'Sister Blackstock, I hear that you've distinguished yourself during this most unfortunate accident. I hurried back as soon as I heard the news, and I'm glad to see that you're quite yourself and making the most of things.'

He beamed around him: 'Temporary, of course; but any port in a storm, eh? We shall be able to get all your patients into St Jude's by the end of the week and your good nurses with them. I hear that a niche will be found for you here until we can get some sort of temporary building.'

'So I'm told, sir.' She didn't smile and she ignored Tane.

'I do feel,' went on Sir Richard, at his most urbane, 'that you should take a day or two's rest, Sister. You had a nasty experience, a very nasty experience—change of scene in which to recover will do you good.'

'Thank you, sir, but I'm perfectly well.'

'You must allow me to be the best judge of that, young lady. Dr van Diederijk has most kindly offered Myrtle

House for your use for two days—he'll be away, he tells me, and I insist that you go there and relax. Doctor's orders.' He turned to his companion. 'You agree, van Diederijk?'

'Indeed yes. Sister Blackstock is more than welcome to rest in her own home. There will be no one to disturb her.'

Euphemia stole a look at him. He looked back at her, his face empty of any expression save one of courteous indifference. She began: 'Well, I…' and was stopped by Sir Richard's upraised hand.

'Not another word, Sister Blackstock. We can't have you suffering from delayed shock, you're far too valuable a member of the staff. Have I your promise to do as I ask?'

Her 'Very well, sir,' was reluctant, but he couldn't have noticed, because he went on: 'I suggest you go there this evening and have the following two days free. I shall mention it to Miss Risby.' He gave her an indulgent smile. 'And now shall we take a look at our patients?'

The round took a very long time because Sir Richard wanted to hear each patient's account of their escape, and as they were all, even Mr Crouch, unanimous in their praise of Euphemia and Dr van Diederijk, she was heartily glad when they at last finished weaving their way from bed to bed, dodging equipment and blankets and screens which the nurses were frantically trying to get into some kind of order. At the door Euphemia, always a tryer, had another go. 'We're in a shocking mess,' she pointed out. 'I really think I should stay—I can take days off later in the week once the men have been transferred.'

But Sir Richard, at his most benevolent, wouldn't hear of it. 'I'm sure that by this evening you'll have everything as you want it and then you can leave your staff nurse to cope for a couple of days; far better for you to be here when the transfer takes place. No, Sister, I must insist that you keep your promise.'

Tane was standing a little apart, as though he didn't care a brass farthing what she did, and probably he didn't. When she peeped at him it annoyed her very much to see the smug look on his face. For some reason he was pleased that she was going to her home, although she couldn't think why, unless it was because she hadn't wanted to go in the first place.

He was a tiresome man and she couldn't stand the sight of him, although she loved him with all her heart. He'd called her darling, too, but she guessed now that that was to get her moving when she had hesitated. She wished Sir Richard a good morning and murmured coldly in the general direction of Tane, her gaze fixed on his waistcoat, and watched the two of them walking away, Sir Richard with his head poked forward and his hands behind his back and Tane beside him towering over him, his broad back very straight. Euphemia, fighting a childish wish to burst into tears, went back to the office where Joan was laboriously sorting the charts which had had to be freshly made out.

'Send the first two nurses to coffee,' she instructed so sharply that Joan looked at her in surprise. 'We'll have ours here—I need it.'

By the end of the afternoon they had wrought miracles. The beds were in some sort of order and lockers had been found for the patients. True, they were scattered all over the place, because Physiotherapy was divided into a number of rooms connected by open doors, and there was

no sluice and only one shower room. But as Miss Risby
had pointed out when she came to see how they were
getting on, it was only for a few days, and most of the
hospital was inconvenienced in some way or other,
although the other wards had got off lightly with broken
windows and smashed furniture. Euphemia, tired, hot, and
keeping her temper on a tight rein, had a job to give a civil
answer, and Miss Risby, who was by no means a fool,
remarked as she left that Sister Blackstock would find
things easier after she had had a well deserved period of
rest. 'Staff Nurse Morris is quite able to carry on for a day
or so and I'll send you extra nurses. Nurse Shotter has
already gone on a few days' leave, hasn't she?'

Miss Risby wagged her dignified head. 'It might have
been a great deal worse, Sister Blackstock, it was a miracle
that the whole of the hospital wasn't involved. And it's very
gratifying to read the account of your actions in the daily
press—and Dr van Diederijk, of course. You've telephoned
your family?'

'Yes, Miss Risby.'

'Splendid, then I must wish you a pleasant two days
at home—it's most kind of Dr van Diederijk to offer it to
you, isn't it?'

'Yes, Miss Risby.'

Euphemia tried to decide whether Tane was being kind
or not as she drove the Morris down to Hampton-cum-
Spyway. She would have liked to have thought so, but she
couldn't think of any good reason for his offer. Aunt Thea
and Ellen, when she had told them on the phone, had been
lavish in their admiration of his kindness. 'Such a good kind
man,' purred her aunt. 'He'll make a splendid husband.'

Euphemia had agreed; it was such a pity that his splendid qualities were going to be wasted on Diana.

She hadn't left the hospital until after seven o'clock and by the time she reached the house it was dark, for there was no moon. She was startled to see a light in the hall and one in the sitting-room, and before she turned the car into the short, drive she stopped it, puzzled. The house was empty, Tane had said so. Her heart tripped over itself at the thought that he might be there, waiting for her. Not that she would be glad to see him, she told herself menaciously, but all the same... She started the car again and stopped in front of the garage, took out her house key and walked up to the front door. She had the key in the lock when she heard Mrs Cross's voice from the kitchen. 'It's only me,' the lady's head appeared round the kitchen door. 'The doctor asked me ter be 'ere ter 'ave a meal ready for yer, Miss Euphemia. Egg an' chips and a nice pot o' tea. By the time yer've got yer bags in, it'll be on the table.'

Euphemia discovered that she was famished and Mrs Cross was a splendid cook and anxious to please. She sat on the other side of the kitchen table, sharing Euphemia's pot of tea, asking endless questions about the explosion.

'Ever so brave, the doctor said. Didn't turn a 'air, 'e said 'e'd rather 'ave had you there than a dozen men.'

'Oh, did he? Did he really? He was pretty wonderful, and I didn't do much, Mrs Cross.'

'That's as may be. Now you go an' 'ave a bath and go ter bed. I'll wash up before I go. And I'll be round in the morning ter tidy up...'

'That's sweet of you, Mrs Cross, but I can manage.'

"'E said I was to. Anyway, I can't come the next day—got ter go ter me sister's, but I daresay you can manage.'

So Euphemia went to her bed and contrary to her expectations, slept soundly until the sun woke her. It was a fine morning and with Mrs Cross there to dust and Hoover she was left with nothing to do but go into the garden. There was plenty to do there; someone had cut the grass and tied up the dahlias and the Michaelmas daisies, but the beds needed weeding, and when she went down to the bottom of the garden behind the hedge she found tomatoes to pick and the place crawling with marrows. She ate her lunch in the kitchen and went back into the garden again and worked there for the rest of the afternoon, so that by the time she was having a late tea she was nicely tired and relaxed. She spent the evening examining the doctor's bookshelves and listening to some of the discs on his CD, and for the second night slept dreamlessly.

She couldn't get into the garden quite so early in the morning, because Mrs Cross wasn't there, and there was her room to tidy and the bed to strip and the house to inspect to make sure that it was exactly as she had found it. All the same, after an early lunch she was ready to go into the garden again, and even though the sun had disappeared and there was a light drizzle, she found plenty to do. No one had remembered the small patch of potatoes; she dug them up with real pleasure and hauled them indoors. It was a pity that in order to get to the store room she had to tramp to and fro over the kitchen floor, but there was no help for it and she could clean it presently.

It was over her tea that she began to feel lonely and sad; perhaps she would never come to the house again, and she loved it so. She cleared the tea things and put them away neatly, then got a bucket and floor cloth, donned an apron of Mrs Cross's and started on the kitchen, floor. She hadn't realised that it was such a mess and she'd have to look sharp if she was to leave in a couple of hours.

She had thought the hard work would cheer her up, but it made no difference. Almost without knowing it she began to cry. She was on her knees scrubbing the worst patches of mud and snivelling, when she heard the front door being pushed open. It would be Mrs Cross, back early and come to see what she was doing. Euphemia wiped her face with the back of her hand and twisted round on her knees.

It wasn't Mrs Cross. Mrs Cross didn't wear enormous, hand-made shoes, well polished, nor did she wear fault-lessly cut trousers and a trendy waist-coat. Euphemia's eyes, travelling upwards, stopped at the firm chin and even firmer mouth above it.

'Oh, it's you,' she said unnecessarily and a trifle wildly. 'You weren't coming back until tomorrow—they said…' She got to her feet and wiped a grubby hand over her tear-stained face again, pushed back her hair and met his eyes.

They weren't cold any more; the blue of them seemed very bright as though he was laughing. And yet his face was almost grim—no, not grim, she corrected herself, tired, bone weary. 'Why did you come?' she asked.

'You silly darling girl,' said Tane softly, 'how can I keep away from you? You're all I want, nothing else matters any more.'

He came towards her, but she backed away. 'Diana…' she began.

'Diana and I broke our engagement two days after we came back from Jerez. She decided that being a doctor's wife wouldn't suit her at all. Cor de Vries will suit her far better—I had hoped that they would take to each other when they met again.'

'You arranged that?' Euphemia was momentarily diverted.

He nodded. 'Well, something had to be done, my darling. I knew that the moment I had set eyes on you driving that ridiculous car of yours, and as if that wasn't enough, fate sent me to Myrtle House—things just fell into place after that, and when I saw you sitting on the stairs eating apples it seemed to me that I would have to give fate a hand, for you looked so adorable. You look quite beautiful now, you know.'

He reached out and plucked her into his arms. 'No, don't try and get away, just stay quiet and listen to me. I've got something for you. I tried to give it to you once and you fell upon me like a wildcat.' She felt his great chest heave with laughter, and he took one arm away and fished a long envelope out of a pocket.

'Here it is.'

It was difficult to open because she had no room to speak of, but she pulled the thick paper out and spread it against his waistcoat.

'It's the deeds of this house…'

'Exactly so, my heart. A wedding present, shall we say?'

She stuffed it back into its envelope and poked it into her apron pocket.

'A wedding present?' Her voice came out a squeak.

He said quite humbly for him: 'If you will marry me,

my dearest Phemie? I love you so very much—I had no idea—life is so very empty when you are not there, I am at a loss how to go on.'

She looked up into his face, and it was all there, just as though he hadn't said a word. In a moment she was going to tell him just how much she loved him too, but first: 'Did you arrange for me to come here?'

He kissed the top of her head. 'It was the only thing I could do, you see I had to talk to you.' He smiled down at her. 'And kiss you...'

He took his time about it, and Euphemia, comfortably aware that there was no need to hide her love, made no attempt to hurry him.

Here's a sneak peek at
THE CEO'S CHRISTMAS PROPOSITION,
the first in USA TODAY *bestselling author*
Merline Lovelace's HOLIDAYS ABROAD *trilogy*
coming in November 2008.

American Devon McShay is about to get the Christmas surprise of a lifetime when she meets her new client, sexy billionaire Caleb Logan, for the very first time.

Silhouette®

Desire

Available November 2008

Her breath whistled out in a sigh of relief when he exited Customs. Devon recognized him right away from the newspaper and magazine articles her friend and partner Sabrina had looked up during her frantic prep work.

Caleb John Logan, Jr. Thirty-one. Six-two. With jet-black hair, laser-blue eyes and a linebacker's shoulders under his charcoal-gray cashmere overcoat. His jaw-dropping good looks didn't score him any points with Devon. She'd learned the hard way not to trust handsome heartbreakers like Cal Logan.

But he was a client. An important one. And she was willing to give someone who'd served a hitch in the marines before earning a B.S. from the University of Oregon, an MBA from Stanford and his first million at the ripe old age of twenty-six the benefit of the doubt.

Right up until he spotted the hot-pink pashmina, that is.

Devon knew the flash of color was more visible than the sign she held up with his name on it. So she wasn't surprised when Logan picked her out of the crowd and cut in her direction. She'd just plastered on her best business-woman smile when he whipped an arm around her waist.

The next moment she was sprawled against his cashmere-covered chest.

"Hello, brown eyes."

Swooping down, he covered her mouth with his.

Sheer astonishment kept Devon rooted to the spot for a few seconds while her mind whirled chaotically. Her first thought was that her client had downed a few too many drinks during the long flight. Her second, that he'd mistaken the kind of escort and consulting services her company provided. Her third shoved everything else out of her head.

The man could kiss!

His mouth moved over hers with a skill that ignited sparks at a half dozen flash points throughout her body. Devon hadn't experienced that kind of spontaneous combustion in a while. A *long* while.

The sparks were still popping when she pushed off his chest, only now they fueled a flush of anger.

"Do you always greet women you don't know with a lip-lock, Mr. Logan?"

A smile crinkled the skin at the corners of his eyes. "As a matter of fact, I don't. That was from Don."

"Huh?"

"He said he owed you one from New Year's Eve two years ago and made me promise to deliver it."

She stared up at him in total incomprehension. Logan hooked a brow and attempted to prompt a nonexistent memory.

"He abandoned you at the Waldorf. Five minutes before midnight. To deliver twins."

"I don't have a clue who or what you're…"

Understanding burst like a water balloon.

"Wait a sec. Are you talking about Sabrina's old boy-friend? Your buddy, who's now an ob-gyn doc?"

It was Logan's turn to look startled. He recovered faster than Devon had, though. His smile widened into a rueful grin.

"I take it you're not Sabrina Russo."

"No, Mr. Logan, I am *not*."

* * * * *

Be sure to look for
THE CEO'S CHRISTMAS PROPOSITION
by Merline Lovelace.
Available in November 2008 wherever books are sold,
including most bookstores, supermarkets,
drugstores and discount stores.

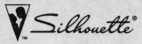

Silhouette®

Romantic
SUSPENSE

Sparked by Danger,
Fueled by Passion.

Lindsay McKenna
Susan Grant

Mission: Christmas

Celebrate the holidays with a pair
of military heroines and their daring men
in two romantic, adventurous stories
from these bestselling authors.

Featuring:

"The Christmas Wild Bunch"
by *USA TODAY* bestselling author
Lindsay McKenna

and

"Snowbound with a Prince"
by *New York Times* bestselling author
Susan Grant

Available November wherever books are sold.

nocturne™

ESCAPE THE CHILL OF WINTER WITH TWO SPECIAL STORIES FROM BESTSELLING AUTHORS

MICHELE HAUF

AND

VIVI ANNA

WINTER KISSED

In "A Kiss of Frost," photographer Kate Wilson experiences the icy kisses of Jal Frosti, but soon learns that this icy god has a deadly ulterior motive. Can Kate's love melt his heart?

In "Ice Bound," Dr. Darien Calder travels to the north island of Japan, where he discovers an icy goddess who is rumored to freeze doomed travelers. Darien is determined to melt her beautiful but frosty exterior and break her of the curse she carries...before it's too late.

Available November wherever books are sold.

MARRIED BY CHRISTMAS

Playboy billionaire Elijah Vanaldi has discovered
he is guardian to his small orphaned nephew.
But his reputation makes some people question
his ability to be a father. He knows he must
fight to protect the child, and he'll do anything
it takes. Ainslie Farrell is jobless, homeless and
desperate—and when Elijah offers her a position
in his household she simply can't refuse....

Available in November

HIRED: THE ITALIAN'S
CONVENIENT MISTRESS
by
CAROL MARINELLI
Book #29

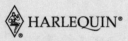

LAURA MARIE ALTOM
A Daddy for Christmas

THE STATE OF PARENTHOOD

Single mom Jesse Cummings is struggling
to run her Oklahoma ranch and raise her
two little girls after the death of her husband.
Then on Christmas Eve, a miracle strolls onto
her land in the form of tall, handsome bull
rider Gage Moore. He doesn't plan on staying,
but in the season of miracles, anything
can happen....

***Available November
wherever books are sold.***

LOVE, HOME & HAPPINESS

HAR75237